ETERNAL LIFE

MARGARITA

"ETERNAL LIFE"
 MARGARITA
Copyright © 2023 Svetlana Kozianenko - Ukrainian Canadian Author,
              Pen Name:MARGARITA.

WICCAN HOUSE/WICCAN KEY
CHURCH ETERNAL LIFE books may be ordered through booksellers or by contacting:
eternallifewiccan@gmail.com

The views expressed in this work are solely those of the author.
Some of the images were produced exclusively by the author.
Any people depicted in stock imagery provided by Thinkstock are models,and such images are being used for illustrative purposes only.Certain stock imagery © Thinkstock.

Canadian ISBN: 978-1-7380559-2-0 (Paperback)

Canadian Library of Congress Control Book Number: 978-1-7380559.

ZZZ

I

This sensational news!
For the first time in the world
published a message from the
Universe, which was not available to
no one scientist!
Ancient gods fly back to Earth!
People previously there was no such
thing as science fiction or fantasy,
people did not invent but only
recorded in the world are the ones
that really happened and they
reflect with using symbols.
Human creator coming back !

BOOK ONE

ZZZ

QUEEN OF THE UNIVERSE

ON THE EARTH

IS AN

QUEEN OF THE CARDS !

ZZZ

The Empress !

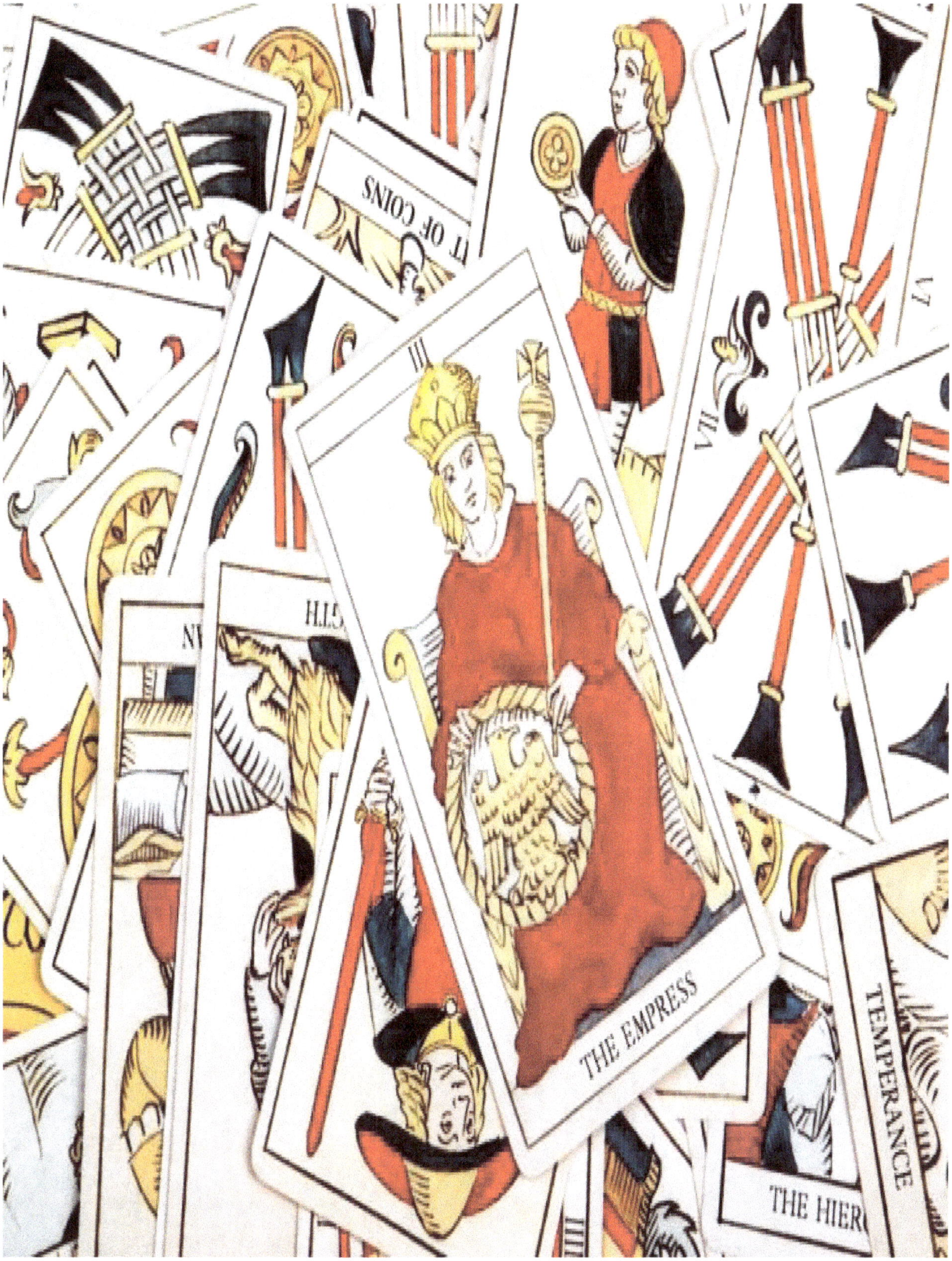
THE EMPRESS
TEMPERANCE

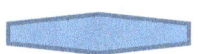

ZZZ

Queen of the Cards presenting the Judgement Day on the Earth , for Paradise and for Hell !

The Judgement !

ZZZZZZZZZZZZZZZZZZZZZZZZZZZZZZZZZZZZZ

The Judgement Day belong to the
Queen of the Universe - the High Priestess,
on the Earth - Queen of the Cards!

The Moon !

ZZZZZZZZZZZZZZZZZZZZZZZZZZZZZZZZZZZZZ

This book was created today are now at the time of Judgment Day and its completion in the world for the living and the dead! Rise up and live and dead, the hour has come! I am High Priestess! I am Queen of the Universe, I imagine all the dead on this Court! On their behalf, I will speak with the living!

ZZZ

What happened on 21st. of December 2012? It didn't end the world. We passed to another Dimension which only me can explain what exactly it is because I came from Paradise and only me who knows the Law of Paradise. I will explain to people, how to come to Paradise, this is my Law, to help to everyone because right now we are in the Hell Dimension. This is the last Dimension before the Paradise, and Paradise is eternal life on the Earth forever!

ZZZZZZZZZZZZZZZZZZZZZZZZZZZZZZZZZZ

The High Priestess !

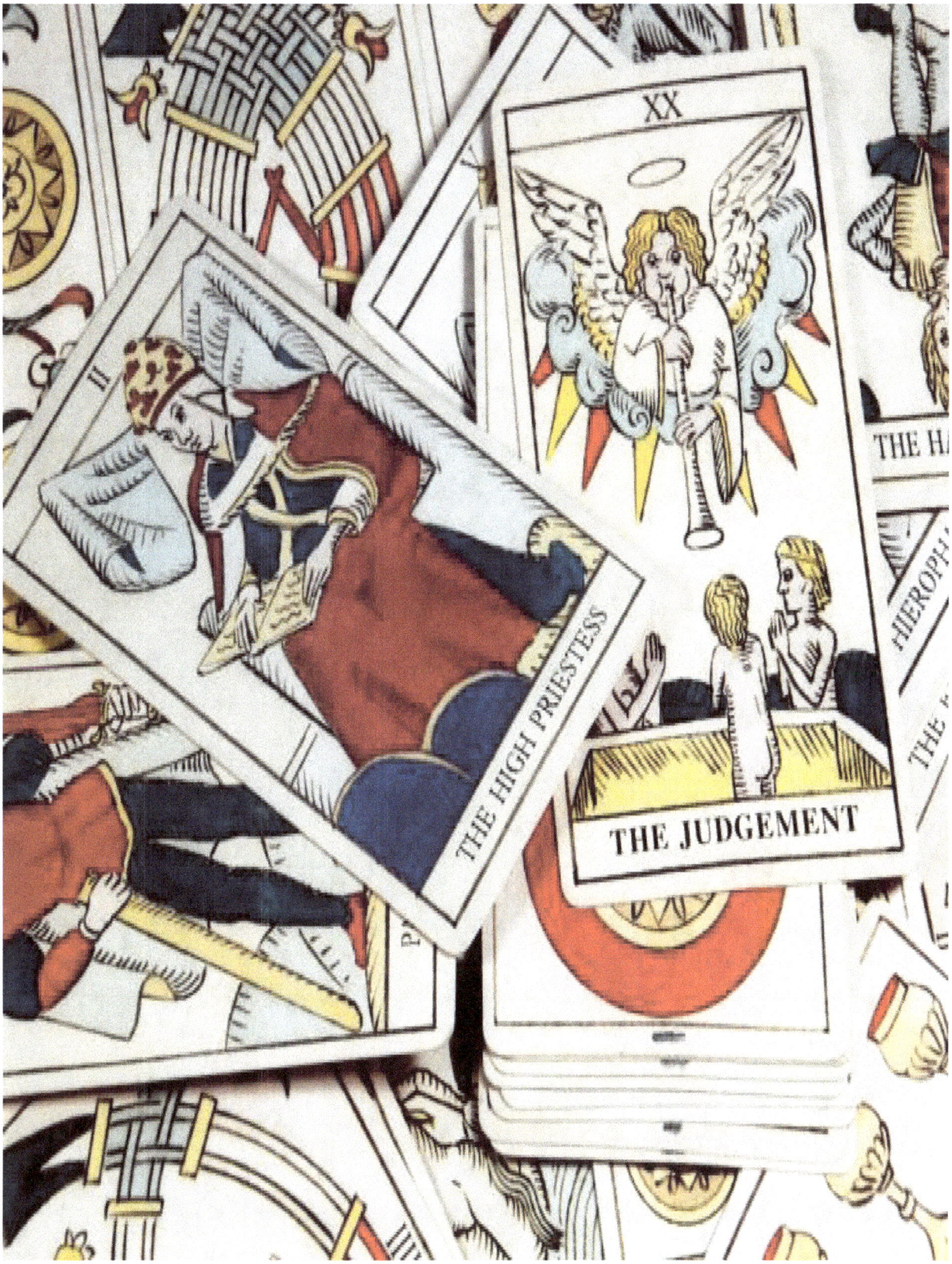
XX
THE HIGH PRIESTESS
THE JUDGEMENT

ZZZZZZZZZZZZZZZZZZZZZZZZZZZZZZZZZZZZZZZ

Wheel of Fortune is my strength and thoughts!

The Wheel of Fortune !

ZZZZZZZZZZZZZZZZZZZZZZZZZZZZZZZZZZZ

II

I declare my will! These cards

represent me!

- ❖ **Queen of Cups Tarot Symbol**

- ❖ **Strength Tarot Card Symbol**

- ❖ **Queen of Pentacles Tarot Card Symbol**

- ❖ **Star Tarot Card Symbol**

- ❖ **Queen of Swords Tarot Card Symbol**

- ❖ **World Tarot Card Symbol**

- ❖ **Moon Tarot Card Symbol**

- ❖ **Devil Tarot Card Symbol**

- ❖ **Hermit Tarot Card Symbol**

- ❖ **Judgement Tarot Card Symbol**

- ❖ **Magician Tarot Card Symbol**

- ❖ **Death Tarot Card Symbol**

- ❖ **Temperance Tarot Card Symbol**

- ❖ **Sun Tarot Card Symbol**

- ❖ **Empress Tarot Card Symbol**

- ❖ **Queen of Wands Tarot Card Symbol**

- ❖ **Justice Tarot Card High Priestess Tarot Card**

- ❖ **High Priestess Tarot Card**

ZZZZZZZZZZZZZZZZZZZZZZZZZZZZZZZZZZZZ

Queen of Cups

ZZZZZZZZZZZZZZZZZZZZZZZZZZZZZZZZZ

Strength

ZZZZZZZZZZZZZZZZZZZZZZZZZZZZZZZZZZZZ

Queen of Pentacles

QUEEN OF PENTACLES

DRYAD

ZZZZZZZZZZZZZZZZZZZZZZZZZZZZZZZZZZZZZ

The Star

ZZ

Queen of Swords

ZZ

The World

400 WORLD OUROBOROS

ZZZZZZZZZZZZZZZZZZZZZZZZZZZZZZZZZZZZ

Moon

ZZZZZZZZZZZZZZZZZZZZZZZZZZZZZZZZZZZZZZ

The Devil

ZZZZZZZZZZZZZZZZZZZZZZZZZZZZZZZZZZZZ

The Hermit

ZZZZZZZZZZZZZZZZZZZZZZZZZZZZZZZZZZZZZ

Judgement

ZZZZZZZZZZZZZZZZZZZZZZZZZZZZZZZZZZZZZZ

Death

DEATH
GRIM REAPER

40

ZZZZZZZZZZZZZZZZZZZZZZZZZZZZZZZZZZZZZ

Temperance

50 TEMPERANCE
SEA NYMPH

ZZZZZZZZZZZZZZZZZZZZZZZZZZZZZZZZZ

The Sun

ZZ

The Empress

ZZZZZZZZZZZZZZZZZZZZZZZZZZZZZZZZZZZZ

Queen of Wands

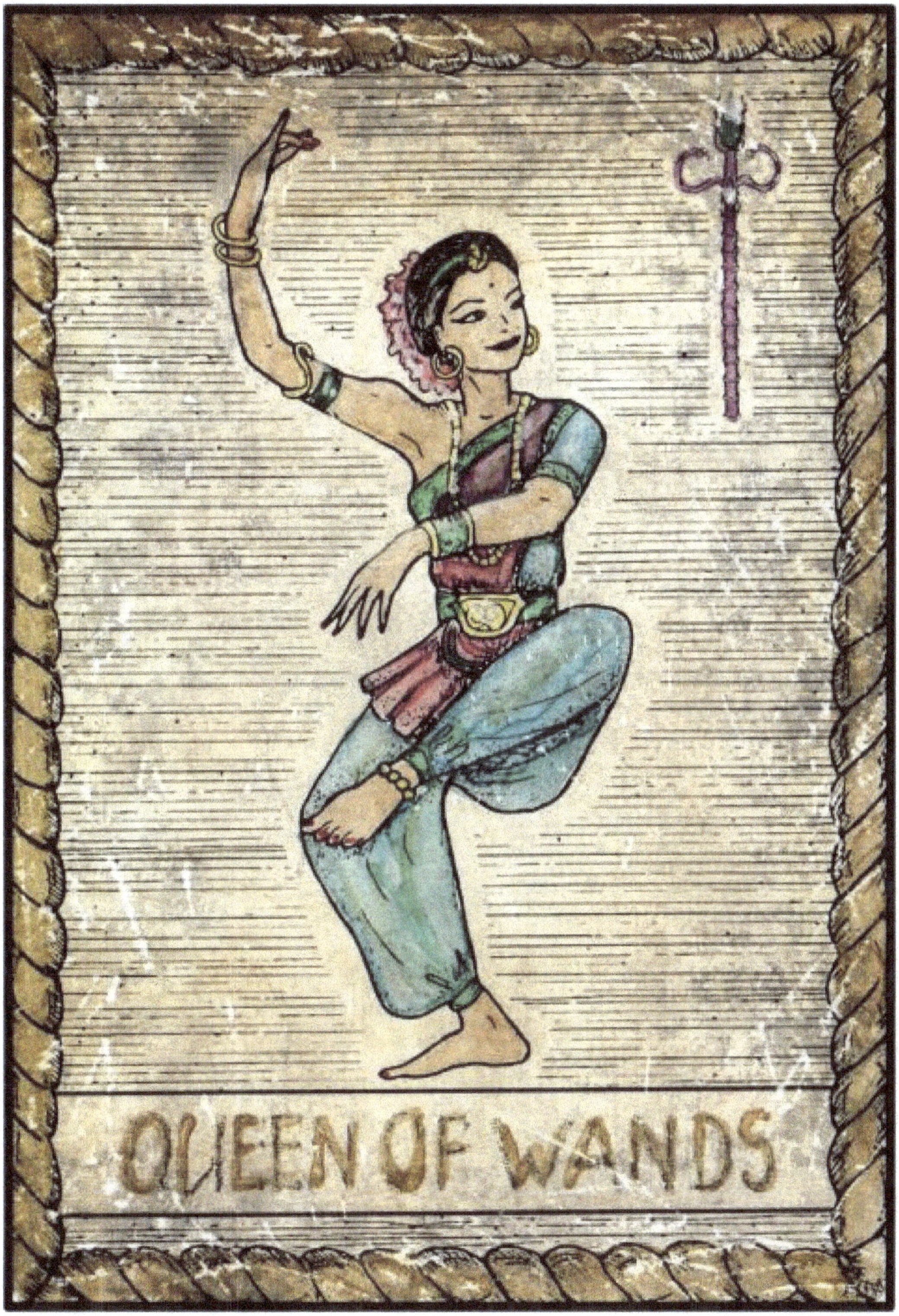
QUEEN OF WANDS

ZZZ

Justice

ZZ

The High Priestess

ZZZZZZZZZZZZZZZZZZZZZZZZZZZZZZZZZZZZZ

Baphomet

Queen of the

Universe-Baphomet

ZZZZZZZZZZZZZZZZZZZZZZZZZZZZZZZZZZZZ

III

Tarot of Black Magic belongs to Queen of the Universe!
These cards present the Law of Love in the Home of the Paradise!
Only arcana of Love belong to Eternity Life!   These cards are cards of Eternity Life!

These cards have the power of ancient magic and remove the hexes of the black Witch! According to the Law of Paradise , I will remove from everyone who will come to me to ask for help for all a curse, mantra, spell and a death hex!

ZZ

The Major Arcana.

ZZZZZZZZZZZZZZZZZZZZZZZZZZZZZZZZZZZZZZZ

The Fool * According to the law of the Universe is an empty man, on the earth, he is the jester . To know him like a serious person in the House of the Universe is ridiculous. Treat it legitimately as not a serious person and in love and in business. Do not continue under the law of the Universe talk about him, he had already stopped as soon as the arcana of the Universe met him. To the person who is a seeker of information for his personal scenario, tell him to stop contact with this person with who he is in the relationship at this time, in order to love the person in whom he will be interested. If THE FOOL falls on the business the relation with this person will need to stop and avoid any relations with him. This man is empty and arcana of the Universe legally do not want to talk with him on Earth.

The Magician * The conversation has to be stopped immediately on the ground with those who taunts the magic arcana universe. The conversation should be stopped as you only learn, when you exit the MAGICIAN arcana, this would mean that the person begging for assistance from you does not recognize contact with the dead, so he does no love for the deceased. With such a man arcana Universe stops contact at once. And you should not continue to deal with this person anymore in the future.

The High Priestess * - is the only judge in the Universe and on Earth. When she arrives, she tells about an important event in a person's life, she tells about the coming of the loved one in your life in the future. Business events are not predicted THE HIGH PRIESTESS. THE HIGH PRIESTESS will belong to only two loving and their relationship in the future, which may not stop and this Alliance ends the marriage. THE HIGH PRIESTESS brings the love and happy family life.

The Empress * - is the QUEEN of the UNIVERSE, the mistress of Heaven and Earth. THE EMPRESS can change laws if there is a need in the House who asks for help. You should ask this person what he needs? And then, when he will tell you about their problem, tell him: go home and don't worry anymore, because everything will change soon and everything will be okay, you will not need to ask help for the second time, and for this reason, because you will no longer need this help. THE EMPRESS of the Universe will bring you peace and love.

The Emperor * - is a God in the world of the dead and to the Earth, he brings love to people in their homes. That love belongs to Heaven and Eternal life. If THE EMPEROR came to you to give help, means in the future, a person will meet his love. Calls for assistance or should leave a relationship with a man who without love and go to the meeting in order to find his loved one. Another law for a person do not. Must be only true love in Paradise according to the law of Eternal life.

ZZZZZZZZZZZZZZZZZZZZZZZZZZZZZZZZZZZZZZ

The Hierophant *, he shall inform about that, this person who came to asking for help there is a problem in love. There he would leave this relationship in the future, with whom it now because this is not a lasting relationship of love. In the future, he will meet their legitimate love. With whom he will live on Earth his entire life and will be registered in Paradise for future Eternal life.

The Lovers * -it's eternal love, which will remain in the Eternal life wherein the Eternity you will stay with your loved one and never be parted again. Where legitimate love will accompany you in your House and nobody will disturb you. You'll be in love and harmony in Eternal life.

The Chariot * warns of alarming upcoming events with your beloved person that will leave you in the future and be with you will never be. The CHARIOT-comes to inform you about this that you will not ever together. The CHARIOT-warns you to know about that and you have to go looking for yourself a real love, and not spend time on an empty love. Since she is already waiting for you so you will love. The CHARIOT already contacted with this person, already reported about you. Wait for meeting with him, because he's already on the threshold in your life. Where will be a house of your eternal love with this person The fate prepared for you real love. A legitimate love, which will remain in eternity.

Strength * Will stop an empty person next to you in your life, where STRENGTH have been seen the empty person near to you who stopping your life, he is an empty man, he is leading a happy life lives near you and using you through your life. STRENGTH will tell you about it and the STRENGTH will not give to laughing at you. Empty love shouldn't be since because you go perish in eternity alone. You must stop empty love and look for those who will love you, for do not stop your life. STRENGTH will not allow an empty love in your home.

The Hermit * said, that the person with whom you are have been met he is empty in love for your home in the future. In marriage with this person, you will not be live and you won't, because his love to you is empty now and he spends time with you and not thinking about marriage with you completely. With such a man better stop communication so as not to lose that person who will love you. This person is already waiting for you because THE HERMIT had already told him about you.

ZZZZZZZZZZZZZZZZZZZZZZZZZZZZZZZZZZZZZZZZ

Wheel of Fortune * reports that you are happy in love and your love is legally owned to the Paradise, to a home of the Eternal life. WHEEL OF FORTUNE came to inform you about that what you are is close to your home with the man who loves you and another would not. WHEEL OF FORTUNE and love with you.

Justice * -reports about the alarm in your home, about the person with whom you're dating, he is cheating you. He has a family and he looking for entertainment on the side of the house with you, hiding his real life from you and mislead you in love with him. This love must be stopped in order do not to stop the love in his home with the person with whom he lives. And you don't wait for to leave him, don't wait for when he himself will leave you and not be disappointed in the fact that you won't find anyone more, thinking that love is a hoax. JUSTICE-tells you: love don't stop there, the people are interested in you. Love and happy family life with that person will be with you.

The Hanged man * Be together you legally, THE HANGED MAN said. Without each other you don't leave so much you love each other, you are inseparable. You are legally in Paradise at the home of the eternal love.

Death * We are talking about the death what belongs to love because you love each other and you are ready to give their lives for each other with your loved one. If it does not become live, and he is gone from the life, love for him will stay with you in your house and you don't give anyone this love in the future. Love with your beloved person will enter in Eternal life and Heaven is your eternal home. Death-Herald of death always comes to your loved one.

The Temperance * -comes to tell about patience, that you need to wait for meeting with your loved one in the future. The person with who you will meet, will with a love for you, which belongs to Paradise and you will go into Eternal life with your beloved man. This is your legitimate love that will belong to you in the house of love, which owns Paradise.

The Devil * -tells you that, what you like to play in an empty love. The DEVIL-tells you, what such a game in an empty love in Paradise will not be in the future. Playing in an empty love this is not legally for the Paradise! It will not belong to the Eternal life! You legally will be stopped and blocked to going to the Eternal life, the Law of Paradise - you will not play an empty game to love in the Heaven!

ZZZZZZZZZZZZZZZZZZZZZZZZZZZZZZZZZZZZZZZZZZZZZZZZ

The Tower * is the home of Paradise on Earth, which is here on the Earth, not in the Heaven. Human happiness and love are here on the Earth, not in the Heaven. Do love here on the Earth, do not look for love in Heaven. In the love we are here on Earth, you are already in Eternal life, nobody will stop you because legally are in the Heaven and Eternal life already here.

The Star * is as a proof of that, what you are in the Heaven here on the Earth, in the legitimate love with your beloved and be move with him in Eternal life. And will be there in love and harmony in eternity, to lose the love you can't never because you are already in Heaven, where love will belong to only two in your House.

Moon * -this is the home of the Universe. Moon-House Universe gives us joy and happiness on Earth. Moon-us connects with the power of love that we get in our House legally on Earth from which we enter into Eternal life. Where love is eternal and loves that MOON has created mankind. The Moon and there's hidden home for humanity, as it has a black magic is the power of love which belongs only to the home Universe. Without the existence of which did not be exist even the mankind on Earth. The Moon will exist in Eternity, and therefore humanity will legitimately exist in Eternity. Moon-comes to tell you that you and your loved one will exist in Eternity.

The Sun * always is happy for people! Sun-legally transfers the warmth of love in your home, for people. The sun comes to tell you that love with your lover may not be without heat. So you are in Heaven on Earth and you will not lose your loved one and go with him in Eternal life.

Judgement * -shall informs you that you will not lose your sweetheart. In the future, you will together be in Eternal life, this is a legally forces the law of Heaven. JUDGEMENT-said, that Paradise is for you with the person your beloved, and in your home in addition to the two of you and your children in it, no one else will be. This is a family in love and harmony, which legally belongs to the Eternal life. Your home will be in eternity dwell in love and harmony.

The World * -tells you not to take advice from the other people about your loved one. People they have different lives and their advice is absolutely not suited to your life. A conversation with the people getting leads to hold your love and you can to lose. Except you and your loved no one should solve your issues - this is the law of Eternal life, which belongs to Paradise. Eternal life in the House, where you are communicating only two, you and your beloved.

ZZZZZZZZZZZZZZZZZZZZZZZZZZZZZZZZZZZZZ

The minor arcana .

ZZZZZZZZZZZZZZZZZZZZZZZZZZZZZZZZZZZZZZZ

Ace of Wands * You will encounter in the future of a loved one, you will not remain one without love. You will meet your legitimate love and will belong to the Eternal life. You will live with a loved one in Heaven in love and harmony.

Two of Wands * Legitimate love together came to inform you TWO OF WANDS. And together, you will be in the Eternal life already here on Earth because you are in the love and harmony with their beloved man.

Three of Wands * -comes to inform you about the appearance of a child with your beloved person. Love gives children of Eternal life. At love to each other will always be children in the Eternal life. Children are the fruit and the joy of love, legally owned by Eternal life.

Four of Wands * On the thoughts and concerns, you have with your loved one-FOUR OF WANDS-tells you about your legit real existence Eternal life love and Eternal life. FOUR OF WANDS-confirms your love, it's your legal love. Love with your beloved person arrives at the home of Paradise. The law of love, which has been ruled by the Eternal life. Love is a House of love.

Five of Wands * says that your love does not belong to the Eternal life in Paradise House. FIVE OF WANDS-informs you that you have to go to a meeting with a person whom you haven't met. That will be your legitimate affection. Only with it, you'll be in eternal love, Eternal life legally in the House. Only with this man, you will be in love and harmony in Eternal life.

Six of Wands * -reports that six-figure is happy in love and belongs to the Eternal life. Six figure proves your existence in Heaven is love and legal residence in the Eternal life with your loved one. This law belongs to you legally with your loved one.

Seven of Wands * -came to announce that in the future you will find your favorite person you'll meet. It takes a long time, but this man will be in the legitimate love with you. With this man, you legally enter into the Eternal life where you'll be in love and harmony. Where the love in your home will be in eternity. Love in the House - is Paradise.

ZZZZZZZZZZZZZZZZZZZZZZZZZZZZZZZZZZZZZZZZZZ

Eight of Wands * says about marriage with your favorite person who will come to you in the future . Legitimate wedding, happy family. EIGHT OF WANDS-informs you that your family unit belongs Eternal life, where a happy marriage belongs to Heaven, where love and is the law. You under the law of love.

Nine of Wands * -informs you that you are happy in your home with your loved one, this is a legitimate love Eternal life where you legally will stay with your loved one. In the House of Paradise that belongs to only two, two people loving each other person. In the House of Paradise, you will never be separated and forever in Eternal life you stay together in love and harmony.

Ten of Wands * - confirms your legal stay in the house of Eden and in the future you and your loved one will legally remain in Eternal life. TEN OF WANDS - a supporting document on the ground in Paradise. TEN OF WANDS - is the passport of love on Earth.

ZZZZZZZZZZZZZZZZZZZZZZZZZZZZZZZZZZZZZZZZ

The Cups .

ZZZZZZZZZZZZZZZZZZZZZZZZZZZZZZZZZZZZZZZ

Ace of Cups * - proves the existence of eternal love lawfully owned Eternal life with the person with whom you live and will go into Eternal life in the future. In Eternal life you will never get lost and will stay together forever in love and harmony.

Ten of Cups * - reports very soon meeting and intimate relationship with the person who will be your lover. In the future, you will live a happy family life. Your love will belong to Paradise, Eternal life. You'll stay in love and harmony for eternity.

Three of Cups * The man who is in the relation with you does not your pair, THREE OF CUPS - came to inform you stop contact with this man, who is now with you. You must stop the relationship with that person. This leads people not serious and empty love with you about the future. Love and family relationships that man has no plans with you. This walk of the person who likes to change partners.

Four of Cups * The relationship you have with your loved one in your home in full understanding and consent of love between you. You are not alone in your House the legitimately love to belong in future abide in Eternal life, where Heaven is love. In the future, you legally in Eternal life-love it and have Eternal life. Where are you in eternity will stay together in love and harmony. Eternal life will save your love.

Five of Cups * The desire to be with you, to love you and be with you in marriage, wants to be with you loved one. A legitimate marriage, marriage proposal soon awaits you. Love with your beloved person legally belongs to Heaven in Eternal life. Were you legally will be in eternity in love and harmony with your loved one.

Six of Cups * -comes to announce that your home is full of happiness and love with your loved one. No one cannot stop your love, so much it strong in your home your love. You and Your House belong to Eternal life, in which you legally reside in the future and legally reside in Paradise in love and harmony in Eternal life. Where never stops loving in your home.

ZZZZZZZZZZZZZZZZZZZZZZZZZZZZZZZZZZZ

Seven of cups * -comes to report that your chosen one with whom you already contact, has a secret from you. Your chosen withheld information from you about that in the future, he wants to get away from you to another man, but he is quietly beside you and is looking for a new contact with the man to whom he wants to go and leave you. Since his love to you already gone, and he's looking for a new love, with which he will do the same as to you. SEVEN OF CUPS-says that such a man empty of love and once you stay without him, do not regret it. This man empty of love, you have to love and be thankful SEVEN OF CUPS , for what she has saved you from future problems, that could happen to you unexpectedly.

Eight of cups * -came to inform you of news, which awaits you in your home. Eight OF CUPS-wants to inform you that, your chosen one having cheated to you, you hope that you will be together in the future and trust him in love with you. Eight OF CUPS-announce that relationship with you no more than a game, which he considers an empty for love and do not create a family. Because it's not going to marry no who, because of his comfortable with free life and not to those who do bind his (her) life. Not to have children and do not even talk about family life in General.

Nine of Cups * -says that no one will be able to put on the damage your love, a conspiracy to death you on your legitimate love, in order to separate you from your chosen one. Love does not stop, it is reported-NINE OF CUPS. Love belongs to Eternal life and there is not a force that can separate the two lovers in Paradise. The power of love without borders is strong, this is her eternity and Heaven will retain the Eternal life of love in your home .

Ten of Cups * -is proof that you have with your loved one together and love each other. TEN OF CUPS-will makes an entry in your book of life in the Heaven, that you are together, and you will be registered at the home of Eternal life and you don't need to because it will have already been completed, and love yours and there is proof of this. That you belong home Paradise and go into everlasting life.

ZZZ

The Swords.

ZZZZZZZZZZZZZZZZZZZZZZZZZZZZZZZZZZZZZZZZZZZZZZ

Ace of Swords * Reports that nobody will prevent you to be with your loved one. In order to enter into marriage and being together, controversial people among your people around you with your loved one is gone. Your love is all around you happy. And everybody wants you to be married to your loved one. In marriage, love and harmony. After marriage, you will go into eternal life and be together with your loved one stay in eternity in love and harmony.

Two of Swords * -says about your joy in the House legal love. Your marriage with your favorite person according to the law of love is owned by an Eternal life where you are with your loved one will be in eternity and eternal life in Heaven in love nobody stops love fails. Love is eternal.

Three of Swords * There is a third man between you with your loved one for whom you still can't be together. Three of Swords reports trouble you to speak on the purity of your beloved that you don't wait until one day when he will leave you and you will be one. Ask him-why don't we get married? And it will not give you the desired response, and then you leave it. Without marriage is not love. This empty craze that is not legally belongs to Eternal life and you will perish. Heaven won't take you lonely.

Four of Swords * Four of Swords confirms that you are happy in love and legally belong to Eternal life and you will be in heaven in Eternal life in love and harmony with your loved one. Love will remain in eternity in your home. Love Eternal life you will always deliver the joy with your loved one. In the Eternal life you'll legitimately is in love together, where love will be your rightful home.

Five of Swords * Be in love you'll-Five of Swords, informs you and the marriage proposal now awaits you. You agree to enter into a legal marriage with your loved one. You'll be together in Heaven and your House will legally belong to Eternal life. Love and Eternal life will keep your House. The law of love in the Eternal life belongs to you two. And your legitimate happiness will always be with you in eternity.

Six of Swords * Stay love funny, don't listen to anyone. Love with your loved one in the future will end the marriage Union. You love each other and you will be together about this came to inform you-Six of Swords. Don't listen to anyone, because you have detractors. You will be together in love and harmony legally belong to Eternal life. Where love is a law and interfere in your home will never be. However, you will be happy and is in Heaven.

ZZZZZZZZZZZZZZZZZZZZZZZZZZZZZZZZZZZZ

Seven of Swords * The fact that you are in love and harmony with your loved one and will be located together in Eternal life - Seven of Swords, came to tell you about it. However, love is in the Eternal life you legally, it confirms - Seven of Swords. Your love is eternal and will not hurt anyone. Eternal love belongs to eternity, and no more than other roads. The law of eternal love is all-powerful and it belongs only to the two of you in Eternal life, it can confirm right now - Seven of Swords. Paradise in Eternal life is a home for people loving each other. In Paradise will continue to Eternal life.

Eight of Swords * Eight of Swords-reports about your lawful existence in Paradise is already known in Eternal life, that the Court has already taken place and love your legitimate happiness in your love with your loved one-Eight of Swords, now gladly announce to you that you knew about this registration. Registration has already occurred, in the future it won't be. You just go to Heaven, following the laws of love where you will find eternal love.

Nine of Swords * Nine of Swords-always comes into the House where legitimately happy in love people. Where the love of two people loving each other belong to Eternal life. Where love two belongs to Paradise in eternity and feelings of love are endless. Eternal life and is called love. Hine of Swords-confirms your legitimate everlasting love.

Ten of Swords * Ten of Swords-reports that love you'll need to meet or already you are together, you should take care now about the existence of Eternal life. To legally register with your loved one in Heaven-the House of love, and then you will legally belong to Paradise-House of love in the Eternal Life. This home of love will be yours legally and you will be in love and harmony in eternity.

ZZZZZZZZZZZZZZZZZZZZZZZZZZZZZZZZZZ

The Pentacles.

ZZZZZZZZZZZZZZZZZZZZZZZZZZZZZZ

Ace of Pentacles * ACE of Pentacles is the home of the Universe and Paradise belongs to all mankind on Earth. ACE of Pentacles is a document belongs to you to be in Eternal life with your loved one. Where you legally reside in love and harmony with your loved one in eternity.

Two of Pentacles * Two of Pentacles-come talk to you, with dedicated pair, which legitimately belongs to Paradise. Where is the power of love and Eternal life in the Universe, and the home of loving people, where the power of love is boundless.

Three of Pentacles * Three of Pentacles. In the House of the Universe will never be the third between two loving people, it tells you the Three of Pentacles. According to the laws of pentacles, the third has no right to discuss any solutions to the problems. that deal only with two loving people.

Four of Pentacles * Four of Pentacles-approve your legal existence in Paradise in the House Universe where love belongs only to you two. And your love in the Universe is not discussed, and never in your life does not intervene. Where you will be together forever in love and harmony.

Five of Pentacles * The man who did you offer that tells you-Five of Pentacles, can't you do not love. Love unlimited, which belongs to the Eternal life. In love and harmony you will live in Paradise with your loved one.

Six of Pentacles * Stop your fate, in which you must have and be with your loved one, no one can. Paradise-the House of love belongs to the Eternal life where people legitimately wish is only in love couples. Do these people even thought such do not exist, to smash the legitimate family alliances in Eternal life. Six of Pentacles is the proof of legitimate happiness in your family in the future, that will be created in love in the House will move Heaven and Eternal life in the future.

ZZZZZZZZZZZZZZZZZZZZZZZZZZZZZZZZ

Seven of Pentacles * Seven of Pentacles-tells you that in the future you will be in Paradise, which belongs to the Eternal life. Where legally you belong to eternal life. Seven of Pentacles-tells you about that in the future you with your favorite person with whom you live out all the happy life on Earth and will go into Eternal life, where will be in eternity legit in love and harmony. Seven of Pentacles is the symbol of the hearth in the Universe, in Eternal life for people loving each other. Seven of Pentacles is a symbol of happiness for lovers.

Eight of Pentacles * Eight of Pentacles-tells you about the future of conversation with your loving you man, about creating a family in the legitimate love with him. You should not refuse, it is your legal fate to him belongs Eternal life. If you refuse him, another such a loving person you like this you will never meet. If you agree, you will be with him in Eternal life is eternal love.

Nine of Pentacles * Nine of Pentacles is a confirmation of your happiness. You must meet in the future. His legitimate love belonging to Eternal life. His legitimate love belonging to family life. Belonging to Paradise, home of love Eternal life. Where you will stay forever in Eternal life, love and harmony with your loved one.

Ten of Pentacles * Message that you in the future with your beloved person will be together on Earth and in Heaven, in love and harmony is in Eternal life, confirms this-Ten of Pentacles. Where you legally will together be marriage and love belong to Eternal life.

ZZZZZZZZZZZZZZZZZZZZZZZZZZZZZZ

The Figures.

ZZZZZZZZZZZZZZZZZZZZZZZZZZZZZZZZ

Page of Wands *   In Eternal life talking about love single people will not be able to open, as lonely in Paradise do not fall. A couple of her you should see on the ground and go into everlasting life together. To you well learned person and have enacted laws of Eternal life, who must take on Earth man, rather than after death. Page of Wands is the human consciousness, which he chooses to Land before going into Eternal life and the law is effective and you live on the land under the law of Eternal life before joining her in universe, and there waiting for your other half to her coming to you because you go there first.

Page of Cups *   Now, what you are together and never be parted again in the future, gladly inform you-Page of Cups. In the future, Eternal life will be forever together under the law of love and harmony. which legally belongs only to you two and you'll be in love and harmony in eternity. Page of Cups-is a dream of two loving hearts.

Page of Swords *   Page of Swords-comes to you when your House is happiness, to tell you that you're with your loved one in the future will always be together. And you never have to be worry about that , what you can be have a problem in love in your home in the future . Page of Swords-always here to confirm your legitimate love with your loved one that you legitimately will be in Paradise.

Page of Pentacles *   Page of Pentacles is the force of life and love, which manages human thoughts. Page of Pentacles-comes to you to talk with him. And to ensure that you asked him to find for you your second half in love, because so far you were alone in your home and Page of Pentacles fulfill your request and you will not be more lonely. You will find true love after talking with the Page of Pentacles. After a week you will encounter your loved one and legitimately enter into Eternal life.

ZZZZZZZZZZZZZZZZZZZZZZZZZZZZZZ

Knight of Wands * Knight of Wands, it is talking about love, about life with you in your House and the loving person you want to meet. Knight of Wands all knows he came to you in order to confirm your desire and Knight of Wands then notifies all your loved one that will come in the legitimate love for you in your home. After the meeting you will be together forever in love and harmony is in Heaven in Eternal life. Disconnect you will not be able to no one because it is the law of love. the law of Eternal life.

Knight of Cups * Knight of Cups happily says that you are not separated with your loved one and you legally belong to the law of love, law of Eternal life and you are in love and harmony with your favorite man in Eternal life. In the House of love in Paradise.

Knight of Swords * Knight of Swords-come talk to you about love in your home. Knight of Swords-wants to tell you about a man who is near you, this man in love with you and this Knight of Swords-informs you about it now. Man this will be with you in marriage. This marriage would belong to Eternal life, you'll be happy. You will be together in Paradise-love in the House.

Knight of Pentacles * When it comes to Knight of Pentacles- he will be talking to you about love, then legally your love with your beloved person will belong to the home of Paradise, as Knight of Pentacles already knows you and he came to rejoice, for you for your legitimate love with which you'll be in Eternal life with your loved one.

ZZZZZZZZZZZZZZZZZZZZZZZZZZZZZZ

Queen of Wands * Queen of Wands-always comes when love between two loving people. Queen of Wands-announces the legitimate love in Paradise, where you will be in eternity with your loved one. The House which will save your love in eternity and you will be together forever.

Queen of Cups * -not possible not to rejoice when comes to you Queen of Cups. Queen of Cups-comes only to those who are in mutual love to tell couples about their legitimate presence in Paradise, home of Eternal life. In the House of eternal love where you will be happy with your loved one.

Queen of Swords * Talk about love came to you , Queen of Swords make and announce that you are not alone will be in the future. Queen of Swords - I saw you in the future with those who love you man, therefore, Queen of Swords came to tell you that you don't get frustrated because you're will be married and belong to the House of Heaven, which belongs to the Eternal life.

Queen of Pentacles * Queen of Pentacles -is a legitimate mistress laws of Eternal life. Love-Queen of Pentacles-never ending to those who love is Eternal life and with the same love Queen of Pentacles can drive out of Eternal life to those who do not believe in Eternal love, which enters Paradise. This word is law Queen of Pentacles for everyone, before you enter into an intimate relationship with your elected representative.

King of Wands * King of Wands comes to inform you that with you is giddy in love man who leads not legitimate love and relationship with you. Illegal in relation to the existence of love, which belongs to the Eternal life. King of Wands wants to tell you about it, so you stopped the relationship with that person and do not fall into trouble with him in the future.

ZZZZZZZZZZZZZZZZZZZZZZZZZZZZZZZ

King of Cups *   You are in a false love, where the about can tell you the only King of Cups which belong legally to Eternal life and has all the knowledge of the rules of love what belongs to Eternal life. King of Cups looks forward to you that you will not continue illegal love.

King of Swords *   King of Swords-is able to recognize your conversations in your home with your choice, you want to stay in the future. King of Swords wants to tell you the details of your conversations so that you do not get into trouble with the person whom you have chosen. King of Swords was not satisfied with the response of love you're chosen by you. Your chosen one makes fun of you, it's a mockery of eternal love and does not belong to the Eternal life.

King of Pentacles *   King of Pentacles, know that your House is love and happy eternal future with your loved one. Your love will not stop anyone dark force power, as the King of Pentacles, it is known that one personality put a spell because you belong to the House of love in Heaven in Eternal life.

ZZZZZZZZZZZZZZZZZZZZZZZZZZZZZZZZ

IV

Queen of the Universe – Great Babylon.

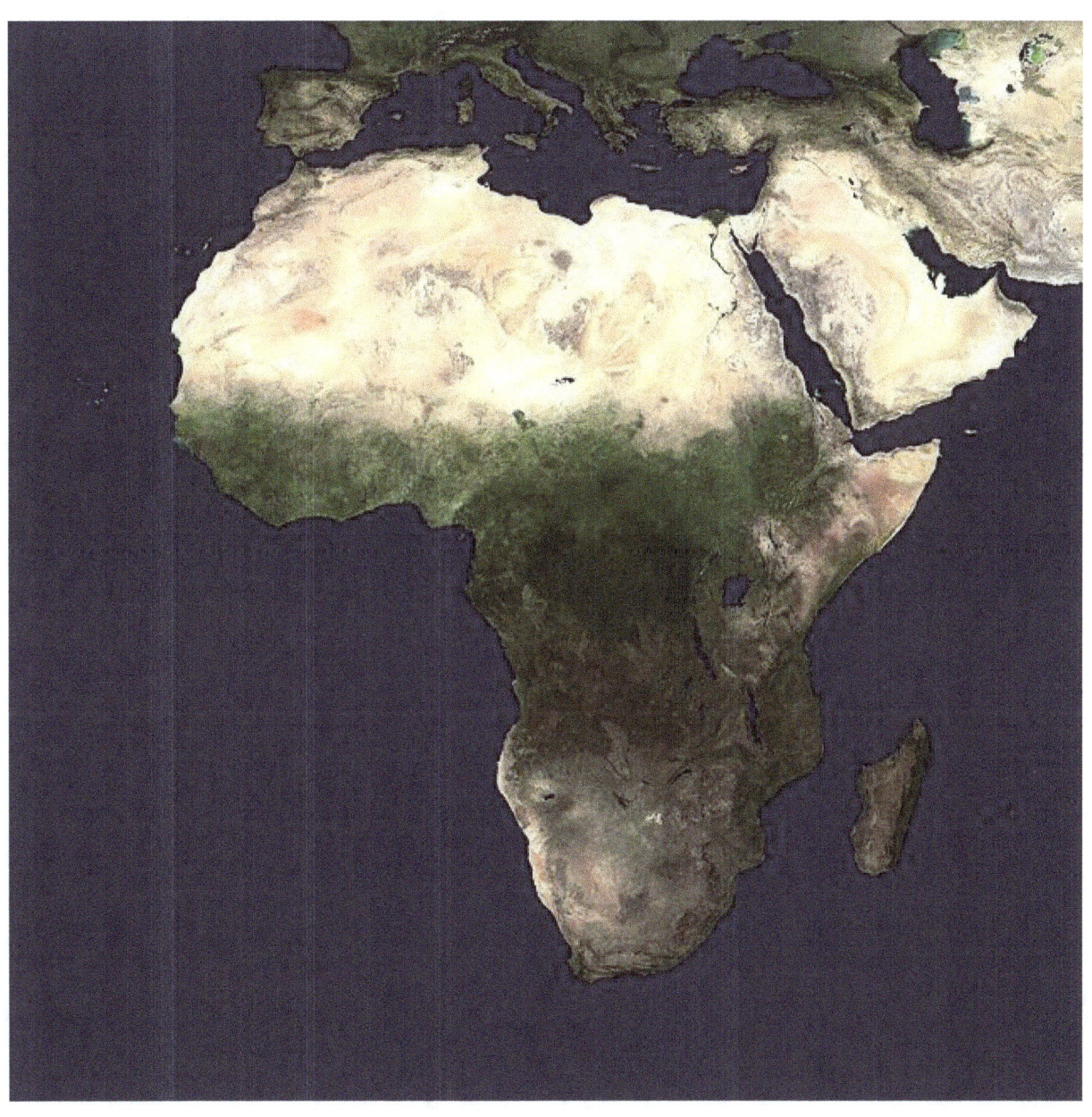

ZZZZZZZZZZZZZZZZZZZZZZZZZZZZZZZ

Queen of the Universe is

a Great   Babylon .

The thought that I was dead didn't exist, I arrived in history as the Great Babylon!

I entered in contact with those men, who know me not to lose contact with them! To build a House that belongs to and will belong to only me and loving me!

Thanks to these people I'm alive and I can talk to you!

In love in my house, that there is simply no such is as Babylon!

ZZZZZZZZZZZZZZZZZZZZZZZZZZZZZZZ

V

Queen of the Universe –

Wiccan Queen.

ZZZZZZZZZZZZZZZZZZZZZZZZZZZZZZZZZ

Queen of the Universe is a Wiccan Queen .

I have successfully arrived in the life of Wicca, to people who learned about the future which I will come to them. These people love waiting for me. The dead were crowned me Queen of Wicca and reported this alive, so today I'm a leader on Earth! Contact with Wiccan people registered in documents of the House of Paradise, legally reside with me and be leaders in Eternal life.

Situs Insulæ Atlantidis, à Mari olim absorptæ ex mente Ægyptiorum et Platonis descriptio.

Africa.

Oceanus

Atlanticus.

Hispania.

Insula Atlantis.

America.

VIRGO

ZZZZZZZZZZZZZZZZZZZZZZZZZZZZZZZZZZZZ

Wiccan Pentacle Black Cat Greeting .

ZZZZZZZZZZZZZZZZZZZZZZZZZZZZZZ

VI

Queen of the Universe – Margarita

"The Master and Margarita"

Mikhail Afanasyevich Bulgakov

The Master and Margarita (Russian) is a novel by Mikhail Bulgakov, written between 1928 and 1940, but unpublished in book form until 1967. The story concerns a visit by the devil to the fervently atheistic Soviet Union.

Published in English 1967 ISBN 1-14-118014-5 (Penguin paperback).

Mikhail Bulgakov

The beginning is near . QUEEN OF THE CARDS ! "Great Ball at Satan's" is done , THE REBORN LIFE AFTER THE DEATH , I'm QUEEN OF THE CARDS and Margarita "The Master and Margarita" . My messenger writer is Mikhaíl Afanasyevich Bulgakov was born in Kiev Ukraine 15 May O.S. 3 May 1891, died in Moscow Russia 10 March 1940 (aged 48).

The novel abounds with Freemason symbols, often showing Freemason rituals which, as the theory implies, originate from the mystery plays of Ancient Egypt and Ancient Greece, Bulgakov had knowledge of Freemasonry. Bulgakov has obtained this knowledge from his father, Afanasy Ivanovich Bulgakov, who had written an article on Modern Freemasonry and its Relation to the Church and the State in The Acts of the Kiev Theological Academy in 1903.

Queen of the Universe.

Queen of the Universe is a Margarita.

ZZZZZZZZZZZZZZZZZZZZZZZZZZZZZZ

THE REBORN LIFE AFTER THE DEATH !!! I'm Queen of the cards, I'm a real Margarita from the 125 years ago from the date of birth Mikhaíl Afanasyevich Bulgakov (15 May O.S. 3 May 1891 – 10 March 1940) was a Russian writer and playwright active in the first half of the 20th century. He is best known for his novel "The Master and Margarita", which has been called one of the masterpieces of the 20th century. Presently on the earth after his death, I will continue to write this novel, to tell in my book about my real past life before when I went on the earth under the name of Margarita! Presently on the earth, I'm Margarita and real Queen of the cards went from the Universe! The universe is my home! QUEEN OF THE CARDS!

Great Ball at Satan's!

Queen of the Universe.

I'm Margarita, the Master's mistress, I was invited to the Devil's midnight ball, where Woland offers me the chance to become a witch with supernatural powers. This takes place the night of Good Friday, with the same spring full moon as when Christ's fate is sealed by Pontius Pilate and he is crucified in Jerusalem, which is also dealt with in the Master's novel. All three events in the novel are linked by this.

Learning to fly and control my unleashed passions. , I entered naked into the realm of night. I was flying over the deep forests and rivers of the USSR and returns to Moscow as the anointed hostess for Satan's great Spring Ball. Standing by his side, I welcomed the dark celebrities of human history as they arrive from Hell.

I never had any problems with a view to come to Earth and become a witch Margarita, and be able to talk with those hermits to the laws of God. Explanation of the existence of God appeared, however, that it was not possible not to understand. Those who had not adopted this law, that simply will not exist and will disappear in the future, that proved the dead arrive at the ball for meeting with me. All of them no longer exist, but the only one I could see them and talk to them. They told me about their pain and inability to return to fix their lives-it was not possible, because each of them has already deliberately elected its path in his life on Earth. So for all this opportunity for them is already locked. All about what they told me has led me in horror, and I did not take them. Talk with them I did not want legally, because it is not according to the laws of Paradise-this was the territory of Hell whence no one and never returned. The door to Hell is locked even for the human brain. All these people will not go out from Hell never and will not return to their family, so how in the Hell people will be too in eternity. Appeal to the God from Hell is not represented.

"Great Ball at Satan's is done!"

My reborn life after the death !

VII

This book was first published, as it contains information from the dead!

The first book in the worlds about the Universe, which I had to publish after coming to Earth!

In the future, while being in communion with the dead, the dead was told me about love in the homes of people on Earth!

I know became from the dead, that they all love Eternal life, which belongs to Heaven and that is the House of love! Existing legally in the future!

These messages I have received from those who have already died and is at Paradise! In the House, where there is no cheating!

Everything about what I will say in my book is a true story!

I must tell you today about my writings!

I have to inform you that the Paradise in the future will actually exist!

I came from the territory of the Universe where the been scheduled Paradise!

Paradise plan inclusive of human existence on Earth is included!

But to realize this plan on Earth, evil Demons stopped my life , me Goddess of Heaven, so do not give me take place on the Earth for to make a happy life for humanity.

I was the only one at that time in the Universe who existed before existence of Planets in the Universe!

On Earth, the dead to me told , me that , I was The Fairy Queen in the Universe!

The Fairy Queen - Queen of the Universe!

VIII

The Birth of the Cosmos, where I Lived   and where was my Home!

I was born in one mighty power space of the Universe connects me to the power of love with the mighty Cosmos grains. And so I was born my soul and Magic Universe was my Home. I talked with auroras around me in the space of the Cosmos.

I have heard it was said to me the space light. We're so good time together and apart from us next time there was no one.

And it was my House where I was happy.

My love to him in the future, they never took and was in the conspiracy, evil Demons were making plans to kill me from the world of the Universe, to pick up the Universe itself. And that I never was able to edit it.

It was the secret plan of evil Demons for coming to Earth on which humanity will exist. Evil Demons have not loved mankind even at this time because mankind was created the magic of love, the love that existed at that time in Paradise and Paradise mankind belongs to Eternal life!

Peace on Earth was destroyed by evil Demons coming from Black Holes in the Universe.

But the power of love in Paradise House is such a strong, those evil Demons his dark plan for the destruction of Paradise in the future will not be able to accomplish! The power of love will not allow because love belongs to Eternal life! And soul under the laws of the Home in Paradise is not dying!

This is the Eternal life which belongs to mankind, which decides the laws of Heaven. And those who do not want to hear about existing laws in Paradise, they will be in the Fiery Lake of fire in Eternity. This is the place which is called Hell according to the laws of Paradise!

Their soul will live, they will hear and see everything , but physically there is nothing they can do because they will be punished for not being adopted by love! For ingratitude to them was given life and they have not adopted these Laws according to which they were born and their soul existed in the Universe before coming to Earth. These people have not enacted legislation under which they were born in the Universe.

And in the future will now be their Court according to the Laws of Paradise! The Court on Earth, when the soul was into the body! That is the proof of the existence of Laws in force in Paradise!

The Sun is a Home of Paradise.

Achievement and proof of the existence of Paradise are a created humanity on the Earth!

And time for the Court in the future will no longer exist. The trial here on the ground after each designate will go in his place in Paradise or in Hell!

On Earth is intended to place of the Court in which the life of each appears in the clarity of its existence!

Therefore, after this Court on Earth, the soul separates from the body and takes her place in the Eternal life!

Or she will be in eternity in Heaven or it will be in eternity in Hell!

This is the Court of Justice on Earth, love according to the laws of Paradise, not dying in eternity!

And I have to inform you that, following the appointment of places in the future, nothing will ever change it will be not possible! And to give help for to change the designated Law for you no one will be !

The territory of Hell and Heaven will not intersect in the spiritual world!

Hell will be separated from the territory of Heaven where there will be souls in love and harmony!

And so will be in eternity!

IX

Election of the Path.

The appearance of space in the Universe has realized thanks to my love for the Universe, which is my soul.

My existence in the world in the Universe is spirituality, which is connected with my heart in my house on the ground, and that is was helped me to have an opportunity to come to Earth and be born a human.

This is a strong spiritual development, to which is equal do not anything!

The Universe is hearing my voice and my home is sending me the information, which was not yet available to humanity before my arrival!

And Dead people with me, all who are already in my house in Paradise, with whom I am in spiritual communion and our thoughts reach leadership achievements in any designated plans in my house in Paradise! Where I like to see people with happy faces, loving and happy in their lives. This life and is called Paradise and another life does not exist anymore. Humanity must know of the existence of Paradise to mankind was the choice and was not without fame. As humanity, another chance in life will no longer be available. Now for humanity on the Earth's is the last chance, because after the death of a man on the Earth will no longer return. And the solution for their choices on the Court people must choose now to not disappear in eternity. Those who do not elect their way he disappears and his name disappears from the book of life in the Universe. And nobody will ever be able to learn anything more. These people should be warned about this in advance, so that they are aware that their waits. And this choice will man must elect and realize that in the future, it does not produce anyone when he will be presented before the Court of his life. So he knew that he would lose in the future his relatives and loved ones. And their relatives to help them assist will not be able to because his name exist will not be there, and so they will not get to Heaven, these people disappear forever from their lives.

This is the Hell were belongs to Queen of the Universe.

Call them they will not be able to because this choice each is personally. Therefore, cherish their own lives and the lives of loved ones not to lose them forever, and then you will enter into Eternal life, eternal love. That exists only in Paradise. Another more simply does not exist. Don't lose your life, do not dispose of your soul, not to lose love. Love belongs to humanity and soul can only love for humanity. Appreciate the fact that you are a man. Appreciate the fact that you live in, this quality is give born love and do not allow check in your soul evil Demons. Then you will love, and happiness will come into your home. Happiness will bring you peace in your life, love will surround you and never more trouble in no way enter into your home. Nothing can become an obstacle to your happiness. Joy and complete feeling of love for each other and obtains the path to Eternal life, which is owned by a home in Paradise. Not happy only people will not be able to buy love. And their House will be closed the door for love. And after the death of change more they can nothing, and will go into the eternal future is already on the path from the Earth! And will be in eternity for its intended purpose, and be able to change their fate, they can no longer because this feature will no longer ever!

Gates to Paradise.

Paradise belongs to the Queen of the Universe.

X

There are no other laws, other than
the law of the Heaven in the Paradise!

If you do not choose your way, you're going to stop and your soul will never acquire the sense of joy. The soul without a sense of joy comes to self-destruction and stop its existence in Eternal life. You have to love your life and fear death because death takes you into eternity and you will not exist in eternity because you will perish forever.

And love you will not find ever, and you will be lonesome. Alone without love in Paradise-place is not assigned!

Place in Paradise is assigned only for those who have already died and expect to love encounters with your loved person with whom they agreed to meet in the world of the dead after death! This is the eternal love being alone to a future meeting with a man who left home in another dimension and was in love waiting for the arrival of her beloved a man in the House of eternal love in Paradise.

Such feelings of great love deliver to couples in love is a joy to be alone, because they know that they will meet. And their life is filled with excessive feelings of love in their lives and they find peace . And nothing will stop their happiness in their lives. No other more laws do not exist, remember only love is the law of happiness in your home. The life of mankind belongs only love and only a loving person belongs to Paradise!

XI

Loving soul in Eternal life.

The law of love which belongs only to the House of Paradise no longer belongs to any other laws that exist in law in the World, not home Paradise. All other laws blocked forever in eternity. Only a loving person has access to eternal life, which only belongs to Paradise and other place does not exist anymore for the existence of a loving soul.

Never forget that another life for the soul does not exist. In an Eternal life without the love is a fall! With do not have the knowledge of love in Paradise should not be archived because there it will be empty and without the meaning into because you are alone. Lonely in Paradise will not be, as in Paradise will all be in pairs.

And only love will give couples Eternal life.

Love will save you in Paradise in eternity and never lose each other. You will be together in Paradise, under the law of love that exists only in Paradise. All other laws are cheating: they tell you that you are in Paradise can be alone and there you will find rest, but this is not the case, as this is a hoax! Without a loved one thought in Paradise even closed!

Don't stay alone, look for your loved one!

Only in couples in love, you'll be in Eternal life happy!

Happiness and love for you the Paradise was have prepared for you!

ZZZZZZZZZZZZZZZZZZZZZZZZZZZZZZZZ

XII

THE LAST TESTAMENT.

The Paradise.

Passport of love.

Registration of love in your book of life is your Passport to you in Eternal life. The Passport of love and give you all the possibilities in your home with your favorite person to deliver joy to you in eternity. That can only make love and nothing else can be so joyful love with your loved one.

And only love is the message of Eternal life!

Last Testament and there is Love!

The last Testament belongs to Paradise!

Passport of love is Eternal life!

XIII

The Hell.

People who do not have Passports of love will go to Hell and will blocked the door to Paradise in eternity. With their relatives in Heaven, they no longer meet too. Lost relatives did not return more than ever. They will be blocked in eternity and their names will be erased in eternity. And you have more of them have nothing to learn. Do not be flippant, know about it now in life that you will never see them all those who lived without love, they will not be with you in Eternal life in the future more than ever. Talk to them you will not be able to ever since they will no longer exist. Bring life back to its something to change, they will never be able to, as they no longer exist. Other life will no longer be given to them and the memory of them, too, will no longer exist.

If on Earth you will be closed from love, and you will be closed.

Talk about love with you is just ridiculous because you laughed at love without taking her on Earth.

Will not believe you in the Heaven, because you can't be able to fool, deceive deceased can no longer because the soul out there and you are surrounded by witnesses who know and have seen everything. And if you disappoint, though known to be immediately and directly to you without confidence, and you will not be in Heaven!

You will find yourself in Hell for laughing over love!

Don't even think about the fact , that were will forgive you all your loving man!

He learns there about you and stop waiting for you and thinking about you.

Do not change the loving you man after his departure from Earth, because you will no longer meet ever for treason in love!

You must be alone in love with loving you man to end your days if you don't want to lose it and want keep your love for eternity. Because without the love , life another no longer exists and your soul will disappear forever.

And you will can't change anything since humanity will already exist in a completely different dimension, which will be located in Paradise in eternity! And time will go only forward, time ago will no longer return. And all will be only in Eternal life in love. And the law of love is the law of Eternal life in Paradise! Only in this way will it be possible to keep love in eternity for those who do not will close from it! To don't believed in it-it's just not possible!

In order not to lose each other , do not stop the feeling of love to each other!

The only Love has been inserted in the commandment in book of life!
Love is all that man needs, the soul without the love, will be simply does not exist!

Therefore, such a person will no longer exist!

Meeting with Dead

in my Tarot cards.

Now I will tell you what happened to me in a past life and how I came to Earth.

My home was the Universe and I met each of the deceased until collected from them with all the necessary information in order to come to Earth.

I'm telling you their names below.

In the 2005 year, I received as a gift from my friend card Tarot. My friend was a fortune teller to which I came to know about my future. Before my arrival in her house, it was already informed, that it will come one of the most powerful Queens that ever existed or will exist in the world of the Living and the Dead! She knew that I was the goddess of Heaven, she had not even looked for evidence and immediately started to talk about my future. In which she saw me the Ruler of the World and the Universe, and know the force of Law, the power of which is no longer available to anyone! The fact that I am in full authority and Leader of the Law of life alive and the Law of life Death, and in the future, I will create Eternal life through communication with the deceased, whom I leaderly available!

And only me they can report information that is not available to mankind! Most inconceivable messages that have been deleted from the mankind still until his appearance on Earth, all the information were wanted to wipe out from you, about those who told you false Law on Earth and announced a lost Paradise! You will learn everything, I'll tell you the whole truth! How I lost my beloved Angel and did everything to come to Earth and find it! In this was helped me my Tarot cards that were at my house!

I laid my cards and a deep sense of love communicating with them affected me from the cards began to receive reports that I have read and understood that mentally through the cards with me tells me a very close person, it was my grandmother died, my mom's mom! My grandma and told me everything, she told me that were she was very waited for this day when I will talk to her, where I will come in the cards! Grandma immediately informed me that what in my House in cards will come to a lot of people from different ancients with which I will communicate in the future! These were people about whom I will announce with pride, with whom I received love and harmony, and messages received from them, which were not known on Earth so far!

Here are their names, leaderly by the law with love of Paradise:

- ✓ Nostradamus (14 December 1503 Julian calendar, France – 2 July 1566, France) . Was an Astrological consultant .

- ✓ Nikolai Gogol (31 March 1809 Poltawa Ukraine – 4 March 1852 Moscow Russia). Was a writer.

- ✓ Jesus (C.4BC Roman Empire Herodian Tetrarchy – C.AD 30-33 Jerusalem, Judea, Roman Empire). Was a central Figure of Christianity.

- ✓ Sergiy Radonejskiy IV century named by name in the World – Varfalamey (14 May 1314 Rostov Russia – 25 September 1392 Trinity Lavra of St. Sergius). Was a Monastic.

- ✓ Elijah (9th. Century BC. Ahab. Israel). Was a Miracle worker.

- ✓ Khayyan Omar (18 May 1048 Iran – 4 December 1131 Iran). Was a Persian philosophy.

- ✓ Pythagoras (C.570 BC. Samos – C. 495 BC. Metapontun). Was an Ancient philosophy.

✓ **Adolf Hitler   (20 April 1889 Austria , Hungary – 30 April 1945 Berlin, Germany). Was a German politician, Leader of the Nazi Party.**

✓ **Dr. Andrei Sakharov   (21 May 1921 Moscow, Russia – 14 December 1989 Moscow, Russia). Was a nuclear physicist.**

✓ **Vladimir Lenin   (22 April 1870 Simbirsk, Russia – 22 January 1924 Gorki, Russia). Was a Russian communist.**

✓ **Joseph Stalin   (18 December 1878 Gori, Russia – 5 March 1953 Kuntsevo, Russia). Was a Central Committee of the Communist Party of the Soviet Union.**

✓ **Mary   (C. 18 BC. Nazareth, Galilee). Was Mother of Jesus.**

✓ **Saint Josef / the husband of Mary Mother of Jesus. (C. 90 BC. Bethlehem – AD. 18 Nazareth).**

✓ **Karl Marx   (5 May 1818 Trier, Kingdom of Russia, German Confederation – 14 March 1883 London, England UK.). Was a German philosopher, revolutionary socialist.**

✓ **Mao Zedong   (26 December 1893 China – 9 September 1976 China). Was a Chinese communist, Marxist – Leninist, Maoism.**

- ✓ **John D. Rockefeller (8 July 1839 New York, US. – 23 May 1937 Florida, US.). Was an American oil industry business magnate, philanthropist.**

- ✓ **Caterina the Great (2 May 1729 Stetin, Russia – 17 November 1796 Saint Petersburg, Russia). Was the ruling Female Leader of Russia.**

- ✓ **Mustafa Kemal Ataturk (19 May 1881 Ottoman Empire – 10 November 1938 Istanbul, Turkey). Was a Turkish army officer, President.**

- ✓ **Alexander the Great (July 356 BC. – Macedon),(June 323 BC.) – Babylon, Iraq. Was a King of the Ancient Greek.**

- ✓ **Muammar Gaddafi (June 7 1942 Libya – October 20 2011 Libya). Was a Libyan revolutionary, politician.**

- ✓ **Leon Trotsky (7 November 1879 Kherson, Ukraine – 21 August 1940 Mexico). Was a communist, Marxist, Stalinism, Leader of Read Army, a Spanish – born Soviet agent.**

- ✓ **Otto von Bismarck / BISMARCK ERA in 1871 (1 April 1815 Germany – 30 July 1898 German Empire). Was a Germany's Semi-parliamentary government, 1st Chancellor of Germany.**

✓ **Napoleon Bonaparte (15 August 1769 France – 5 May 1821 Saint Helena, UK.). Was a military and political leader.**

✓ **Kossack Mamay (Zaporizhian Sich, Ukraine) in 1775 is a Ukrainian folkloric hero.**

✓ **Nestor Makhno (26 October 1888 Russia – 6 July 1934 Paris, France). Was an anarchy-communist revolutionary.**

✓ **Vladimir the Great (C. 958 Pskov, Russia – 15 July 1015 Berestove (Kiev) Ukraine). Was a Grand prince of Kiev, Ukraine.**

✓ **Saint Nikolai Velimirovich (4 January 1881 Serbia – 18 March 1956 Pensylvania, US.). Known as the Chrysostom. Was a Holy Bishop.**

✓ **Muhammad (C. 570 CE. Mecca, Saudi Arabia – 8 June 632 AD. Medina, Saudi Arabia). Was an Islamic Prophet "Muhammad the Apostle of God".**

✓ **Gabriel Who typically serves as God's messenger (17th - century passenger galleon, see Gabriel "Ship").**

✓ **L. Ron Hubbard (13 March 1911 Nebraska, US. – 24 January 1986 California, US.). Was a Religious leader of Scientology Church.**

- ✓ **Mikhail Afanasyevich Bulgakov (15 May 1891 Kiev, Ukraine–10 March 1940 Moscow, Russia). Was a Russian writer. He is best known for his novel"The Master and Margarita", which has been called one of the masterpieces of the century (ev. of Babylon).**

- ✓ **Michelangelo di Lodovico Buonarroti Simoni (6 March 1475 Italy – 18 February 1564 Italy). Was a sculptor, painter, architecture and poet of the High Renaissance.**

- ✓ **Wolf Messing (10 September 1899 Warsaw, Poland – 8 November 1974 Moscow, Russia). Was a clairvoyant, telepathist, hypnotist.**

- ✓ **Edgar Cayce (18 March 1877 Beverly, Kentucky – 3 January 1945 Virgina Beach, Virgina). Was a mystic, clairvoyant.**

- ✓ **Grandmother Vanga or Vangeliya Pandeva Dimitrova (31 January 1911 Strumica, Ottoman Empire – 11 August 1996 Sofia, Bulgaria). Was a blind, clairvoyant, mystic, herbalist.**

- ✓ **Alaric King (370 Peuce Island, Dobruja – 410 Cosanca, Calabria). Was a King of the Visigoths.**

- ✓ **Peter the Great or Peter Alekseyevich Romanov (9 June 1672 Tsar dom, Moscow of Russia – 8 February 1725 Saint Petersburg, Russian Empire). Was a Tsar Peter I of all Russia.**

✓ **Nickolay Alexandrovich Romanov (18 May 1868 Saint Petersburg, Russia – 17 July 1918 Yekaterinburg, Russia). Was a Tsar Nicholas II of Russia.**

✓ **Grigiri Yefimnovich Rasputin (22 January 1869 Seberia, Russia – 30 December 1916 Saint Petesburg, Russia). Was a Russian peasant, pilgrim, mystical faith healer, and trusted friend of the family of Nickolas II , the last Tsar of Russia.**

✓ **Judas Iscariot   (died C. 30 – 33 AD.). Was an according to the New Testament, one of the twelve original disciples of Jesus Christ and son of Simon Iscariot.**

✓ **Aleksandr Solzhenitsyn (11 December 1918 Kislovodsk, Russia – 3 August 2008 Moscow, Russia). Was a Russian novelist, historian and short story writer.**

✓ **Alexander Pushkin (6 June 1799 Moscow, Russia – 10 February 1837 Saint Petersburg, Russia). Was a Russian poet, playwright and novelist of the Romantic Era. Founder of modern Russian literature.**

✓ **Richard Evelin Burd   (25 October 1888 Vinchester, Virginia – 11 March 1957 Boston, Massachusetts). Was an American naval officer who specialized in feats of exploration.**

- ✓ Heinrich Khunrath (C. 1560 Dresden, Saxony – 9 September 1605). Was a German physician, hermetic, philosopher, and alchemist. Heinrich Khunrath's "Amphitheatrum sapientiae aeternae" of 1585 (Duveen D 897 Flat). The Duveen collection was acquired by the University of Wisconsin to enrich its library holding in Support of historical studies of science and technology.

- ✓ Albert Einstein (14 March 1879 Kingdom of Wurttemberg, German Empire – 18 April 1955 New, Jersey, US). Was a German-born theoretic, physicist, philosophy of science.

- ✓ Charlie Chaplin (16 April 1889 London, England – 25 December 1977 Vaud, Swizerland). Was an English comic actor, filmmaker.

- ✓ George Washington (22 February 1732 Virgina, British America – 14 December 1799 Virgina, US). Was an American solder and statesman who served as the first President of the United States.

- ✓ Julius Caesar / Gaius Julius Caesar (13 July 100 BC Rome - 15 March 44 BC Rome). Was Dictator of the Roman Republic, Consul of Roman Republic.

✓ John F. Kennedy (29 May 1917 Brookline, Us – 22 November 1963 Texas, US). Was an American politician who served as the 35th President of the United States.

✓ Mikhail Vasilyevich Lomonosov (19 November 1711 Denisovka, Russia – 5 April 1765 Saint Petersburg, Russia. Was a Russian polymath, scientist and writer, natural science, physics.

✓ Marilyn Monroe (1 June 1926 California, US – 5 August 1962 California, US). Was an American actress and model.

✓ Charles Darwin (12 February 1809 Shropshine, England – 19 April 1882 Kent, England). Was a best known for his contributions to the science of evolution.

✓ Winston Churchill / Sir Winston Leonard Spencer-Churchill (30 November 1874 England, UK – 24 January 1965 England, UK). Was a Prime Minister of the United Kingdom.

✓ Mary the Magdalene (Born Magdalene C. 4BC. Judea, Died – France). Mary Magdalene traveled with Jesus as one of his followers.

✓ Marc Chagall / Marc Zakharovich Chagall (6 July 1887 Vitebsk, Russia – 28 March 1985 Saint-Paulde-Vence-France). Was a Russian nationality, later French. Painting, stained glass.

✓ **James Springer White** / also known as Elder White (4 August Palmyra, Maine – 6 August 1881 Battle, Greek, Mi). Was an author and co-founder of the Seventh-day-Adventist Church. Husband of Ellen G. White.

✓ **Ellen G. White** / Ellen Gould White   (26 November 1827 Gorham, Maine – 16 July 1915 Elmshaven, California). Was an author and co-founder of the Seventh-day-Adventist Church. Wife of James Springer White.

✓ **Pastor Russell** / Charles Taze Russell   (16 February 1852 Pennsylvania, US – 31 October 1916 Texas, US). As an American early 20th century Christian restorationist minister, Bible Student movement.

✓ **Joseph Smith**   (23 December 1805 Wormont, US – 27 June 1844 Illinois, US). Was a religious leader and founder of Mormonism.

✓ **Martin Heidegger**   (26 September 1889 Baden, German Empire – 26 May 1976 Germany). Was a German philosopher.

- ✓ **Elvis Presley (8 January 1935 Mississippi,US – 16 August 1977 Tennessee,US). Was an American singer and acter.**

- ✓ **Duke Mikhail Illarionovich Golenischev-Kutuzov (16 September 1745 Saint Petesburg, Russia – 28 April 1813 Bonzlau, Prussia. Was a Field Marshal of the Russian Empire. He served as one of the finest military officers and diplomats of Russia under the reign of three Romanov Tsar: Catherine II, Paul I and Alexandr I .**

- ✓ **Nikola Tesla (10 July 1856 Smiljan, Austrian Empire – 7 January 1943 New York, US). Was a Serbian-American inventor, electrical engineer, mechanical engineer, physicist, futurist.**

- ✓ **Baruch Spinoza (24 November 1632 Amsterdam, Dutch Republic – 21 February 1677 The Hague, Dutch Republic). Was Dutch philosopher of Sephardi / Portuguese origin.**

- ✓ **Johne Lemon (6 November 1754 - 5 April 1814). Was a British Wing Member of Parlament.**

- ✓ **Solomon (C. 970 – 931 BC. Jerusalem). Was a King of Israel.**

- ✓ **Johannes Valentinus Andreae (17 August 1586 Herrenberg, Duchy of Wurttenberg – 27 June 1654 Stuttgart). was a German theologian, who claimed** to be the author of an ancient text known as the Chymische Hochzeit Christiani Rosencreutz *anno 1459* published in 1616, Strasbourg, as the Chemical Wedding of Christian Rosenkreutz.

- ✓ **Rudolf Steiner / Rudolf Joseph Lorenz Steiner (27 February 1861 Austria-Hungary - 30 March 1925 Dornach, Switzerland). Was an Austrian philosopher, social reformer, architect and esotericist. Steiner founded an esoteric spiritual movement, anthroposophy . With roots in German idealist philosophy and theosophy; other influences include Goethean science and Rosicrucianism. Lucifer-Gnosis-issued by Rudolf Steiner in the name of Lucifer was understood as a Symbol of knowledge and Light.**

- ✓ **Leonardo da Vinchi (15 April 1452 Republic of Florence/Italy – 2 May 1519 Amboise, Kingdom of France). Was an Italian polymath, art, science. Movement High Renaissance.**

- ✓ **Rembrandt / Rembrandt Harmenszoon van Rijn (15 July 1606 Leiden, Dutch Republic - 4 October 1669 Amsterdam, Dutch Republic). Was a Dutch painter , biblical and mythological themes as well as animal studies.**

- ✓ **Emperor Maximilian I, Holy Roman Emperor (22 March 1459 Inner Austria - 12 January 1519 Upper**

Austria). Was King of Romans the first Renaissance monarch of the Holy Roman Empire.

✓ Conrad Celtes (1 February 1459 Franconia, Germany – 4 February 1508 Germany). Was a German Renaissance humanist scholar and Neo-Latin poet.

✓ Johann Reuchlin (29 January 1455 Pforheim, Germany - 30 June 1522 Studgart, Germany). Was a German-born humanist and a scholar of Greek and Hebrew, whose work also took him to modern-day France, Austria, Switzerland and Italy.

✓ Albert Durer (21 May 1471 Holy Roman Empire - 6 April 1528 Holy Roman Empire). Was a painter Engraving. Movement High Renaissance.

✓ Al-Rashid of Morocco (Tufilalt, Morocco – Died 1672 Marracech, Morocco). Was Sultan of Morocco.

✓ Paracelsus / Philippus Aureolus Theophrastus Bombastus von Hohenheim (11 November 1493 Swizerland - 24 September 1541 Austria). Was a Swiss-German philosopher, physician, botanist, astrologer and general occultist.

✓ Mary I of England / Mary Tudor (February 18 1516 at the Palace of Placentia in Greenwich, England - November 17 1558 St. James Palace in

London). Mary Tudor was the first queen regnant of England and Ireland.

✓ King David (C. 1040 BCE Judah, Israel - C. 970 BCE Judah, Israel). Was the second King of the United Kingdom of Israel and Judah.

✓ Alexander Sergeyevich Griboyedov (January 15, 1795 Moscow, Russia - February 11, 1829 Tehran, Iran). was a Russian diplomat, playwright, poet, and composer. He was Russia's ambassador to Quajar, Persia.

✓ Jan Baptist van Helmont (12 January 1580 Southern Netherlands - 30 December 1644 Southern Netherlands). Was a Flemish chemist, physiologist and physician.

✓ Nicholas Culpeper (October 18, 1616 London, United Kingdom - January 10, 1654 London, United Kingdom). Was an English botanist, herbalist, physician and astrologer.

✓ Johann Georg Faust (C. 1480 or 1466 – c. 1541). Was an itinerant alchemist, astrologer, and magician of the German Renaissance.

✓ Sultan Moulay / Rachid Ben Cherif (Tafilalt, Morocco – 1672 Marrakesh, Morocco). Was Sultan of Morocco.

All these famous people in the history of humanity continue to be in touch with me! Stop communication with them is not possible, they like to chat with me!   No longer exists on the Earth people like me to whom the deceased come in contact with love and understanding, telling me about people!

XV

The spirit of the Devil

came into my   cards Tarot.

My life stopped in mind when I saw in my cards sent me a message from the Devil, which so far have not seen not one person who could come in cards to him! All those whom he met earlier, people who have come to ask the Devil for help, all these people were without love and their desire to get help from the Devil ended mockery on the Devil and not thanks for helping them. So the Devil stopped feeling sorry for people and he stopped coming to their aid. And it disappeared in so hopelessness after they cheated and he lost his beloved in the Universe, even before the humanity appeared on Earth.

Find him in the future coming on earth could I, I looked for my beloved, who disappeared then from me in the Universe.

And we met and had not anything, that can interfere with our feelings of love!

But he began sternly, for do not get into in his house for someones.

1 October 2006 Montreal, Canada.

Midnight : his appearance was in

the abyss of death, in the bowels of the absorption depth of the Earth. View the cover without the feeling the force to survive, while over land that depth abyss collapsed from the pressure of the invisible forces of the spirit of the Devil I have under my feet. And I was on weight over this deadly spot from which there are no easy ways and opportunities to escape from there. Speed collapse of stones from the walls of the depths of the Earth was like the wind.

    The Devil was silent, he only sent the force of fear to me and kept me on the weight over abyss death. But I was absolutely sure that he loved me and would say about this myself, and I've been waiting for having stayed on weight over his prepared the death trap for anyone who comes to him. When he saw that I don't have to see him evil and fear to die in this abyss because I'm not guilty before he is not what and was complete with an open mind and not trying to look for no salvation because I knew that he was my soulmate. He is my favorite which I lost and I found, but at this point, he has not a clue about it. And I gave him to understand if he wouldn't guess who I am, then I will give him my life he can now very easily to wall up me under the ground at such depth from which never out, and nobody there will never find these possessions of the Devil. I gave him to understand that I will not go up from this place as pointless for me to leave him and I didn't have to leave him. I was ready to give him their life forever. The Devil saw this and guessed, that was I am because the force of love as with me could not be longer with anyone. After he lost me in the Universe, the Devil was under the Earth. Alone and suffering, he waited for the Court on the ground when I will be on the land, I will come and find him. Waited for the Court on which he wanted to tell the whole truth about what happened when he lost me. And here is the at last

he asked me;

The Devil: "you came here to see me why?"

I am: "I looked for you all this time after we got lost. I finally found you my love and now we will be together forever in Eternal life with you and nothing can longer ever again what can disconnect us."

-When he heard my words spoken, his heart unblocked and he couldn't keep his feelings to me that he was felt to me in the Universe, in our House where we lived in oblivion love the infinite before we came to Earth.

He told me:

The Devil: "my lovely, you are my only, for me except you nobody no longer exists, I'm forever yours. We are a husband and wife now according to the laws of Paradise in the Universe, and from that moment we don't leave with you ever. And you're legally joining possession of my Black Magic forces in eternity.

You are the Empress in the Universe in the World of the Dead. You're legitimate and the only Empress in Eternal life. And only you has right to contact with the dead, which I saved and protected to loan the day on Earth.

Now the World of the Dead belongs to you. And you can proceed to the beginning of the trial, to ensure that everyone knew what path he chose, and you will write down this designation in their book of life. In this, I will not participate, because I am so tired of the suffering of being without you. The dead will tell all you themselves their thoughts are clean, they will not be able to lie. This is all loving people who are in the Act of love in Heaven in Eternal life. Go and get, my lovely, all these people I guarded and maintained their calm on the Moon. They are buried on the Moon. They waited for all this time you saved them and their loved ones. Go meet them, they like you! "

   -And I mentally went to the Moon, without lingering for a moment not on the spot, and not leaving it to the future of this very important information for me and for those people who were there already millions of years and have experienced excruciating suffering in anticipation of my coming for them on the day of the Judgment Day on Earth.

   - When my appearance of their graves was reeling from my mental touching to him on the Moon! All of these people in these static graves in one voice that made him pierced me sound, passing me their deepest suffering from exhausted in their century-old graves, they told me;

   Dead: "we love you!

   We know that you will come and rescued us do that no one else can! And take us to his house where we will not suffer from the torment. And we meet up with their favorite the missing with which we have been missing. And will live in eternal love not knowing suffering anymore. "

   -And at this point when they spoke to me, I saw how moved soil on the Moon which was covered by a sand to cover the grave of each human being and maintain invisibility located cemetery on the Moon from all those who came to the Moon.

And all those who had the opportunity to visit the Moon were dead, and those who was survived has not the capacity to get to the Moon in the future. The Devil has blocked access to the Moon because it is his home and he belongs only to him and his beloved to me, legal according to the Laws of the Universe. And he happily at our meeting on the ground told me that, it is your house my lovely and besides to you, he does not belong to anyone anymore. And now you're legitimate mistress all Darkness in Eternity! Only you are my favorite do know the Laws Secret World which is not available to humanity even in their minds! And after your appearance on the moon will be completely stopped access to information on the Moon!

Legally, all the forces of the Moon on Earth belong only to you! A love like yours does not have any more! And legally dead love you and come to chat only with you! Your only love they know, this love for them is so much which is no anymore with the one else!

And I released all who was in those graves on the Moon. There were people who were killed and painful death they are beloved lost on them. All of these deaths were missing and suffered the loss of their loved ones. They all cleared for today and are in my house in Paradise! I am in contact with them and they say to me completely with an open mind to me and nothing to hide! I have no problems to access any information with them! And all the people already I took from the grave to the Paradise and the wind where was carried sand on this place where was put in the waves, reminiscent of the waves of the sea and left wavy surface at the site of graves.

And after I released all of the deceased I get fell to the ground mentally at the home now in our House with the Devil. To be together and continue our conversation about us since our separation in the Universe, our conversation lasted ten years since our meeting on Earth. During this time I was able to find all those people who separated us. Who got hiding all this time and changed their names from the mankind on Earth for to be never learned the truth and not learned about who actually is the Devil. In order not to lose power over their non-existent law with the dark forces in Paradise, which they created and still do not stop to go against the law of Eternal life. It's ridiculous to look at how they go without stopping, knowing that Judgment Day will be! On the Day of Judgment you will not be able to lie! You personally will speak for yourself, where the brain will be in such an aura that will create an atmosphere in which you will speak only the truth, you simply can't control yourself. Only your memory will be able to tell about you for all your lived life. At this moment your soul will be separated from the body. The soul reproduces memory and can speak without your body. Therefore, the eternal soul and soul appoints the Judgment Day for the fact that humanity does not believe in Eternal life. And on the Day of Judgment, all those who do not believe in Eternal life will be sent to Hell!

In Paradise, they will not fall for the fact that they ruled the Earth knowing that they should not have done this. And so those who knew and did forbidden acts on Earth they will not even be admitted on the Day of Judgment since there is nothing to talk with them about.

They separated us and the deceased told me that hypnosis had been put, this power of thought which always belonged only to the universe, that is to my house and the power of hypnosis belonged to love. Dark forces then put a hypnosis on him and hid it in their dark thoughts. And it took me only time to come to Earth and find my beloved, it took several tens of millions of years. Because without my beloved Eternal Life can't exist. And I told all the dark forces that if I do not find my lover I'll stop the whole World! Dark forces from the Universe are the souls of already dead people, those that existed earlier on Earth. They told me that they would do anything to help me find my lover. Their promise I got in the Universe before I came to Earth. All the dead who are in my house in the Universe can't refuse me anything. They receive information from the Earth only from me. Any incoming information from other persons sending it to my house, the deceased, is not accepted until the Day of Judgment begins. The day in which everything will turn out and torture no one will come, and many will disappear just in eternity.

This law I appointed to all those who wanted to hide from me in eternity my beloved, whom I found under the ground. But no one else can stop the power of the Eternal life of the soul except me. And for love to each other, we are ready to die! Such a power of love we have, that we can't replace each other with anyone! We both were waiting for this day on Earth to meet! The Devil has never interfered in the conversations of people before meeting me on Earth! The Devil only waited for me to meet with me and suffered from anguish being under the ground alone! He knew that love is eternal and it is not possible to get lost in Eternal life, in which he alone believed! And nothing will stop all the witnesses who were attended at the time of the creation of the World! And the power of the magic of love belonged to both of us alone, the power that will exist in eternity! A law that obeys only Love! And in the law of love, there is no limit! The humanity which was evaluable to separate us, to them this power of love was not available! They laughed at our law and separated us so that the law of love did not exist anymore because for them it is ridiculous. They did not accept this law because they do not accept love with one person in eternity. They have chosen the way to laugh at those who love them and avoid the next and the next people for marriages, to change them and not to remain with the same and the same person in their lives. So they planned in eternity, thinking that they could stop the force of the laws of Paradise and continue to rule the World. Those who know what love is, are not capable of such actions! Therefore, there also witnesses who can't remain silent! Love will not stop them, and for being living in love in their home in Eternal life they told everything that happened to us and why they put hypnosis on the Devil!

Eternal love is the Wheel of Fortune which is Eternal Life, which belongs to Paradise!

These people were the witnesses of our separation on Earth, there in Heaven, we were in love and harmony. Conspiracy to separate us with the Devil, dark forces conceived in Heaven in my house in the Universe. They wanted to stop our love and separate us in order to rule with the dark forces that they wanted to use against the law in Paradise. The law of Paradise was to exist on Earth with humanity! Secretly from me, the dark forces before my arrival on Earth deceived my Devil, they told him that he must go to Earth first without me. They told him that I would come to him on Earth soon after him, And they told him not to worry since I would never leave him, that my love for him is very strong and I can't live alone without him. The Devil could not disbelieve them because in a house in the Universe he had never encountered deception with the dark forces. After the Devil descended to Earth, he has never seen or heard of me since. The Devil believed in our love and knew that I would come after him to Earth and find him. He knew that the dark forces would not be able to lie to me because they loved me. They themselves will tell how they deceived the Devil. As Lucifer was meeting a snake and not me, and only from one glance at her, he realized that he had been deceived by spirits, whom he always trusted in our house in the Universe. Where always in love and harmony lived before he came to Earth and he closed his soul from them forever. He realized that instead of me they sent a snake to Earth and in the future, on Earth there will be no love that I bequeathed to the future mankind. Love on Earth could not be without my presence! And the joy in the life of humanity will be stopped, since we were separated and now only the court is needed on Earth!

Lucifer is not guilty of anything and about this, you will only learn today after 78,000,000,000 billionth. years from the date of the appearance of mankind on Earth who was subjected to the destruction of their life on Earth by dark forces using hypnosis to destroy Paradise! To do this, they needed Lucifer for to use him!

All the witnesses came, both alive and dead, in order to stop the deception that the dark forces reassured Lucifer in his life! In court, the deception will be revealed and in the future, there will be no obstacles in love with us. After the trial, evil spirits will not interfere with our lives anymore, they will be mentally expelled from the Earth and Paradise will come on Earth! Because we have met and will be together, and the Earth will be saturated with our love, and humanity will legally pass into the dimension of Paradise on Earth, and will remain in love with all those in their homes who will mentally expel evil spirits from themselves and their loved ones in their lives and lives Close. For those who will not cast out evil spirits from their life on Earth, they will be legally stopped already on the Earth, even before he leaves his life, he will already be blocked from access to those people who will be in love and harmony. His life will be alone until the last day before leaving Earth and after that, his life will disappear forever, the memory of him will disappear from all those who knew him! Only those people who in love and harmony will live until the last day in their life on Earth are lawful in Paradise and will pass to Paradise after leaving Earth at the time of death!

XVI

Black Magic belongs to the Universe of my house!

The Universe consists entirely of Black Magic, which consists of the feelings of love belonging to my home of the Universe! Only in the Universe are these feelings, since there are no other dimensions in the world where Black Magic could exist! Black Magic is not available to anyone since it belongs only to me and the Devil! To the humanity, Black Magic is not available, because no one has the knowledge how to use it! This knowledge in the mankind has not been laid since the creation of the world on Earth! For the fact that evil spirits used the power of hypnosis and stopped the Devil's brain thinking ability forever. The snake's eyes hypnotized Lucifer when he looked at her, thinking it was me. And Lucifer, from that moment on, did not say anymore with anyone over until today. He was under the earth and waited when I find him, to speak Lucifer only wanted with me. 78 000 000 000 billionth. years his life was taken away from home, was separated from me and without the opportunity to go to Earth to people, since the way out from under the Earth where he was immured by a stone wall in the territory of Israel. People who did it then did not want his appearance in life more than ever. Knowing that the Devil belongs to love in a house in the Universe, magical love, the love that belongs to Eternal life with me. And my love, those evil spirits wanted to stop to my Devil, too, they stopped my life before I came to Earth. Their plot was transferred to Earth to their people who came to Earth according to their malicious plan and they ruled the Earth for the first 3,000,000 years. On Earth, all this time lived underdogs who illegally captured the Earth. Underdogs received information from his man from the planet Saturn that he would come to Earth in the future as a god and his name would be Zeus. According to the instructions of the future plan for Earth from the god Zeus, the underdogs produced a sucrafaiting of my life, so that in the future nobody recognized me. They took a goat and cut off her head, then mentally imagined a female body that had a head from a killed goat. By this ritual, the underdogs created a goddess who does not exist in life ever, who in future came into their house as not being in real origin ever as a symbol of Baphomet. After that, they bowed to the stone wall under which the exit for the Devil was grounded to Earth from under the Earth. And in the future, they never told anyone about their malicious plan that no one would ever know and did not guess what they were planning, that they keep Lucifer under the Earth, whom they deceived when they told him to go first to Earth. After that, Lucifer lost the opportunity to communicate with his beloved and had no opportunity to contact me from under the Earth, since he no longer trusted the dark forces after they deceived him. And without the slightest pity for Lucifer, after they lived a soul in the soul in the Universe before they came to Earth, they took and immured him underground. For his love and sincerity for them, these people threw out Lucifer from his house from the Universe in order to master the house of the Universe. And to be closer to me, since I alone rule the laws of the Universe and they want to prevent the possibility of bringing Lucifer back to me. Since together with him, we will return to Earth the lost Paradise, even then created by me on Earth. And with me, they wanted to talk all the time and their stories would lead only to future promises, which throughout the future would never have been true. Therefore, they began to use the Black Magic on Earth, which belongs to love and not to them!

Therefore, Black Magic does not work here on Earth. The power of Black Magic bears only fear in man, this fear can mentally stop a man's life, therefore a man before the force of fear feels like hopeless because the strength of the spirit of the human brain is not protected from fear. Therefore, only the person himself participates in this at the moment of his own desire to get in touch with the mental conspiracy that these people created to create fear for humanity in the future for those who want to know the Black Magic. They gave a fairly serious formulation in their schemes in order to believe in the Black Magic, which is invented by these people and is used only by these people. In houses where darkness reigns and they wear black clothes on which we can recognize them. And to talk with these people is about nothing because they ignore us in their lives completely. And they will never be hospitable to us in their home, as they need to keep a secret about the buried under the ground of Lucifer so that this information be not available to no one person who has no knowledge of secret information. Where inside of the subconscious, each of them has the knowledge that they hold the Angel under the ground who loved and was not fallen, but he was simply immured underground. But Lucifer's soul is eternal and his eternal love for me is not separating us. I know all the thoughts that not one person knows and so I found my Angel Lucifer, who was my Devil, my husband in the Universe. After that, the attackers began to use the Devil on Earth as a force of fear of humanity, the fear of which never existed. Their plan was to completely confuse people so that people would never know who was talking about. And there were no more pleasures in life in the houses of mankind either, their plan was to destroy humanity, their plan that humanity would not exist anymore. This is not Lucifer's hatred of people, Lucifer is very fond of people. For people Lucifer never did anything wrong, this plan of evil spirits from the god Zeus from the planet Saturn, Zeus created a system of destruction of mankind and passed this system to his people on the planet Jupiter. Only this people know the secret plan from the planet Jupiter so that humanity will never exist and they willing to continued to take possessioned of the planet Earth. For to stop these people who continue their malicious plan against humanity, will only love them, the love which they were deprived of yet in the Universe. Then when I planned to create humanity they decided to send me revenge, because I want to exchange them for humanity. Therefore, they created a plan for the destruction of mankind and for to stop this plan of destruction of mankind in order to preserve Eternal life on Earth, not only for people but also for them, will only love on Earth to those who live in this society next to us. Talk to them about love, not about destroying this society, then people will reach the highest sense of the relationship in love on Earth, everyone who loves them. Then the love for them will help you to understand this society, why it is and why they want to destroy Love and not give it on Earth to mankind. After all, they were temporarily left by me while I was busy creating the Earth. People from the planet Jupiter did not agree to remain without me even for a moment. Their relationship with me did not provide an opportunity for separation since our love with them was also planned for the future. Therefore, these people wanted to be beside me not apart and participate in the structure of the future Paradise on Earth with me together. Therefore, when I told them to wait here for me in the Universe, because there will not yet be no Earth, not people, and when I create the opportunity for life, then I'll call you right away. But for people from the planet Jupiter this time seemed very long and they decided that I did not love them. And then they informed god Zeus on the planet Saturn that he would stop love on Earth so that it would not get to people because I left people without love on the planet Jupiter. Therefore, they came to Earth to prove their love for me and their devotion, as in a house in the Universe to me, even before the advent of mankind. Therefore, they keep humanity in their conspiracy, which does not allow for love, so that the court they want's to begins and they want me myself to come and find Lucifer on Earth, and on the Day of Judgment, they will tell me about their love for me and how they got to Earth. That's why they made Baphomet out of me so that I could find them myself, so only I can know their secrets and they will also know that I found them myself.

And then their life will change when I tell them how I love them and how I did not have them in my soul and I was lonely without them. But now I'm here with love on Earth and with love, we will talk together about Eternal life, and the Universe where there is a world of the dead is now available in the forces of knowledge and humanity on Earth. And Paradise which was lost on Earth and not got to humanity will be found and legally will belong to humanity on Earth in Eternal Life. Thanks to the dead and my love for them, Paradise was found and declared to humanity. The territory of Paradise in the future will be liberated in 350 years and given to people, and only then humanity will go to a new dimension in Eternal life. On that day, there will not be one more person without love. Love will be the law in Eternal life and these people will go to Eternal life. And the house of Eternal life for them will be in eternity.

Where love will inherent in their homes and they will reunite with their loved ones in the world of the dead, where the communication of the living and the dead will not have a difference in existence between the living and the dead. This is the Eternal Life, which people so expected.

God Zeus from the planet Saturn told people on the planet Jupiter, that he would come to Earth.

ZZZZZZZZZZZZZZZZZZZZZZZZZZZZZZZZZZZZ

The Queen of the Universe is the beloved goddess of a secret society!

The creation of a horoscope has secret information in which my personal data belonging to me was laid when I come to Earth!

To hide me from people, I was created the head of a goat Baphomet and by this plot, constellations were created in the Universe, and later a horoscope where I am Aries in order not to lose contact with me, and to wait in the future for meeting me because they really love me. And they know that this secret will be known only to me alone, the Universe brought me to Earth under my designated zodiac sign on the date of my birth on April 17, 1967, of birth. And then we finally meet joyfully in love and harmony in order to talk about what happened then in the Universe with them. And after that, the Judgment Day will be completed and the Eternal Life will enter its reign, which should have happened even then on the first day on the Earth of its existence with the first mankind. The law which is authorized only to me, since there is no other power in my house of love in Paradise belonging to Eternal life, no longer exists.

Aries

Scheme of the secret sign of the zodiac that belongs to me is Aries.

After this, the animals were used by other civilizations by assigning symbols to them.

After that, all these animals came to Earth to people in order to distract me from attention. All these animals were enclosed in a circle so that I would not stand out and thus people from Jupiter could have a connection with me.

*12 signs of the zodiac, they are a

*12 Greek gods ancient, they are a

*12 apostles. The Apostolic Age of the history of Christianity is who were come to us on the Earth, the names of the twelve disciples of Jesus are Peter, James (the son of Zebedee), John, Andrew, Philip, Bartholomew, Thomas, Matthew, James (the son of Alphaeus), Thaddaeus, Simon the Zealot and Judas Iscariot. Dating from the Great Commission of the Apostles by the risen Jesus in Jerusalem around 33 AD. The apostles are our messengers to the Universe from Earth to support communication with the house from which mankind originated and appeared.

*The house for the Earth was the star Sirius, this is one of the brightest stars in the Universe.

* Where I lived all this time before coming to Earth because I was not at home after I was left alone without my beloved. I was left alone without a home and without friends, my star helped me to find contact with people where I used my own forces that belonged to Black Magic in order to obtain the necessary information for me from living people from Earth and from the dead from the Universe. Therefore, I have all the information About what happened in my house!

But for me to be able to come to Earth, I had to create people from the star Sirius, with whom I came here. We are all of one blood in order not to be lost to us in the future. And besides us in helping each other, no one can help us, since we all have one blood group, which is a negative rhesus factor. Scientists are aware of this rare blood group, which belongs to these unusual people. As for me.

* The Greek god Zeus (3rd. century BC. and the Indian god Manou-Maisei (dates from circa 100 CE), who came to the Earth illegally and brought false information into the houses of people, the information that stopped human life on Earth, are brought before the court!

*Alexander the Great was a King of the Ancient Greek (356 BC.), Alexander broke the power of Persia in a series of decisive battles, most notably the battles of Issus and Gaugamela. He subsequently overthrew Persian King Darius III and conquered the Achaemenid Empire in its entirety.[b] At that point, his empire stretched from the Adriatic Sea to the Indus River. He sought to reach the "ends of the world and the Great Outer Sea" and invaded India in 326 BC, winning an important victory over the Pauravas at the Battle of the Hydaspes. Alexander died in Babylon in 323 BC, the city that he planned to establish as his capital, without executing a series of planned campaigns that would have begun with an invasion of Arabia. Alexander's plans followed the Babylonian events and after his death ruled by the Diadochi, Alexander's surviving generals and heirs.

*King Tutankhamen (or Tutankhamun) ruled Egypt as pharaoh for 10 years until his death at age 19(C.1346-1328 BC.). His rule was notable for reversing the tumultuous religious reforms of his father, Pharaoh Akhenaten. Tutankhamun left from the Earth to the Moon, his body was transferred with the help of Black Magic. The Devil made of him a stone statue, which he kept until the Day of Judgment, which will begin on Earth after my arrival. And if I do not talk to Tutankhamun at the trial, it means that it will not be possible to understand what happened to people not understanding what is the Black Magic, which was only available to him then on Earth when he was there. He could talk to the Universe and then communicate with people, as people used to believe in the past. He was a powerful magician and no equal. In the houses of people, he was a lord, healer, and fortuneteller. To stop it and for today is not possible, a statue of Tutankhamun speaking, which is to the Moon. There, on the Moon, his tomb is torn in which he will rest in eternity, except his one there on the Moon is no one else. My Black Magic he will now be kept for me there on the Moon and come out to me for contact when I call him to fulfill my order!

People are forbidden to come to the Moon!

Queen of the Universe.

* For a long time, historians of science have argued that the focus of world culture was only in Africa and Asia.

* Historians of astronomy believed that their science originated in the countries of the Middle East (Babylonia, Assyria, Egypt), as well as in ancient China and India.

* However, in the last decades, this view had to be reviewed, since another cultural center was opened. He was located in the territory of "New World" - in Central America, on the lands now occupied by Guatemala, Southeast Mexico, and British Honduras.

* Particularly interesting is the Yucatan peninsula which was once inhabited by the Maya Indians who created their own distinct culture.

Ancient of the Aliens.

Ancient of the Egypt.

 -Events of the Babylon.

The end of the World on December 23, 2012. the end of the current calendar cycle also marks the start of the next one rather than an onslaught of the apocalypse.

Mayan Calendar:

It is NOT "The end of the World" - but the end of an "ERA" !!!!

 We passed to another Dimension which is the Eternal Life from now and forever!

Queen of the Universe.

♠ Eternal life is Eternal Black Magic!

♠ Queen of the Universe in a life of the Black Magic is a Queen of Spades!

Record by Queen of Spades belongs Queen of the Universe! Witch Queen of the Cards belongs to the house of Black Magic in the Eternity Life!

❶

With love and understanding with the deceased, who are in my house of Black Magic in the house where I am the Queen of Spades. Only I own the language of Black Magic and no one else!

Eternal life belongs to the Black Magic and the secret of the existence of the Black Magic in Eternal Life is known only to me and no one else!

Humanity will never suffer from the Black Magic! Black Magic is love, love belongs to the house of the Universe from which comes the power of Black Magic, thanks to which the Earth and humanity were created! And there is no other power that created the Earth and humanity!

Black Magic connects humanity with the Universe, through which everything lives!

Black Magic is life and love, belonging to humanity on Earth!

In the house of the Black Magic on Earth, I the Queen of Spades I connect humanity with the Universe, from where everyone who loves or wishes to meet love, I will help you to get to Eternal life, since until this time this path was closed and about Black Magic was spoken of as death that scared of people. The Black Magic in the Universe was called Lucifer's love for me since we lived on the Moon! Our home was the Moon, which gave us this love! Legally, I am the mistress of the Moon! **2**

The Moon! belongs to me, everyone in the Universe knows about it, all the dead that belong to the world of the dead and the world of the dead belongs only to the Universe, where humanity legally has no access to the world of the dead!

In the world of the dead, I am the Empress and associate with everyone who comes here after death!

From the world of the dead man goes to the destination in his life from Earth!

The High Priestess the Queen of the Universe.

"Church of Eternal Life"

17 April 1967.

XVII

"Paradise is Lost" - the lost will to the Earth, which I left to people

And I want to tell you about this ....

The creation of life took place in the space age. It is a cosmic union of the UNIVERSE, not an explicable magical power. And the energy of the soul of the UNIVERSE, which belongs to the female likeness. This energy has occurred with the accumulation of time - it is the force of air from the natural compounds of positive and negative connections. And for the initial time, the UNIVERSE did not have a haven. She was tired of excessive space and was looking for a way to stop, and have a HOME!

The soul of the UNIVERSE was so powerful that it already foresaw the FUTURE in which humanity and ETERNAL LIFE were conceived.

And then the soul of the UNIVERSE gave impetus to the materialization of her design!

This was the proof of the original birth of the WORLD!

The regularity of the cosmos is as follows: the energy of the UNIVERSE is reunited with cosmic dust. And then came the birth of the feminine principle in the cosmic life in which the plan of man was laid.

And after the conceived, the POWER that created mankind appeared!

But one of the first was the Divine appearance of the woman MYTH from the materialization of the UNIVERSE energy, which became the MISTRESS OF THE SKY! More than that, for that initial time, there was not naturally more anything. There was only the cosmos that created this woman MYTH with her energy, and with the help of space was formed from the cosmic material for billions of years of the PLANET OF THE MOON! The energy of the cosmos PLANET MOON was very fond of and the development of the first PLANET was in mutual agreement with the energy of the cosmos. With the accumulation of time, the PLANET OF THE MOON was completely formed and then the life force appeared in the MOON - ENERGY, which in the future created a PLANETARY FAMILY. And they existed as one family with PLANETS: PLUTON, NEPTUNE, URANUS, SATURN, JUPITER, VENUS, MERCURY, MARS, and SUN.

And since the power of the MOON was in the guise of a woman, simultaneously with the PLANETS, she created herself a couple - a man whom she conceived at the time of the CREATION OF THE WORLD from her original design.

Successful completion - and the female look from the MYTH, ruling on the MOON - is turned into a GODDESS who became a hostess of this PLANET. A man created her ANGEL. And their COURSE is done on HEAVEN in eternity in the UNIVERSE in love to remain and youth. So they enjoyed the unbroken magical connection. And they were with the ANGEL there alone, and the PLANETS. There was one single family - until the formation of the PLANET, which at that time still could not do anything because of their incomplete formation - in integrity.

Just like the MOON, it had its original origin in space. And then they all needed a future because they are all alive, and the GODDESS - the MASTER OF THE MOON is their creator!

The newly appeared PLANETS arrived alone. And unlike the MOON, they needed a creator who would give the future to all of them! The PLANETS sent a bellicose alarm - the COSMIC WAR began!

MOON won because only she had the most powerful energy. If there is a pack of energy, not one of the PLANETS can win! Such power simply does not exist! To surpass this power is not possible, she is the CREATOR - THE GODDESS OF THE MOON!

Winning a PLANET WAR, the space family called the winner EMPRESS! Since it was so powerful on the PLANET OF THE MOON - MAGIC OF LOVE, REVIVAL AND DEATH IN ETERNITY IN POWER! She rules the LAWS of SKY and nothing else can exist. It is simply not possible and its ages are not calculus, they are stopped in ETERNITY because time is not countable in space!

PLANET OF THE EARTH did not exist then. And the first nine PLANETS remained empty. Therefore, the EMPRESS created the EARTH on which you could be live! Since these PLANETS were not suitable for life. PLANETS had to remain alone until the creation of people on EARTH. But the EMPRESS was never able to come to EARTH to create mankind since a secret conspiracy took place in the space family by which those who organized it came to EARTH before the EMPRESS to the ready EARTH that the EMPRESS had prepared for the people.

By secret conspiracy, these aliens had a plan by which they should not allow the appearance of mankind never, that never happened on EARTH.

Therefore, they created their man on the PLANET OF THE EARTH, he was Adam, he was alone since there was no one other than him on the EARTH then. And then thought those forces who created their own man that he needs a woman to create a family and to create a future generation on EARTH. But to continue their malicious plan was not possible, because in the space family in the UNIVERSE it became known that they deceived the EMPRESS and are on the ground. After that, the EMPRESS secretly turned into a woman in order to stop this plan of intruders and that no one recognized it came on EARTH, calling himself EVE.

The interest of the EMPRESS was to create the humanity that she so dreamed of on Earth where she could live with her ANGEL next to the divinely created people with whom she wanted to communicate and be with them together in ETERNAL LIFE!

Attackers never found out that this woman was EMPRESS. The purpose of the EMPRESS was to teach Adam that he should have a family that would be his home with his wife and future children. In the family, he must remain forever together without betraying his wife in the future. And the EMPRESS came to EARTH in a terribly ugly image, small, with a growth from a lilliputian, and disabled, limping on one leg, with a large and skewed face and with a dominant character. EMPRESS came to EARTH specifically in such a terrible shape that Adam did not fall in love with her. Since she was then only the only woman on EARTH. And the EMPRESS was very fond of her ANGEL, and in her plans was to find her missing ANGEL on EARTH, in what future people who will contact her will help her.

And mankind appeared after the EMPRESS created people by design. She created a woman for Adam the way he wanted and six more pairs. Happy couples to Adam and his wife were not lonely and they were all at the age of 33 to which belonged to her ANGEL. This age has chosen the EMPRESS, in which mankind is able to love. It is at this age that people on the EARTH learn and confirm themselves. And all these pairs that created the EMPRESS were very happy on EARTH.

For more evil forces were not able to, besides how to send their man to EARTH, in order to create humanity they do not have such strength and knowledge for this.

The only deception was inherent in them, nothing else they could do, using their ill-intentioned plan in the future on EARTH. Before the advent of Adam and the first people on the EARTH, in order for the EARTH to be able to live in the future for mankind has taken 7 days to create EARTH.

In the likeness of his space family, the PLANET OF EARTH was created. Living material from space in conjunction with the most powerful energy of the EMPRESS for 7 days created all life on EARTH. But in the first days except for stone, dry soil and 7 pairs on EARTH then nothing else existed. The sun was shining without a halt, the heat was hot and there was no water.

On the territory of PALESTINE, the first people were formed in the first three days. Primordial humanity had a dark skin color.

After that, when everything was ready, the EMPRESS left EARTH and returned to the UNIVERSE, where she had to spend billions of years alone because her ANGEL was not with her in the UNIVERSE.

Therefore, the EMPRESS was in the cosmos disguised so that no one would recognize it until it came to the EARTH in the future.

Therefore, the prevailing power of darkness in space gives fear to mankind in order to stop them from appearing in space and to make it clear to people that I myself will come to EARTH. But evil forces did not stop and were looking for how to destroy the first Primordial people on EARTH.

Evil forces sent a snake to the Garden of Eden which was called the PARADISE where these first-born happy couples lived. In the GARDEN of EDEN, which belonged to these first people, this GARDEN was their home so that they could exist before they settled on the EARTH. It was a PARADISE GARDEN, in the GARDEN it was possible to feed on these PARADISE APPLE FRUITS that gave them strength for life.

But the snake penetrated this GARDEN and hypnotically told people not to eat the fruits in this GARDEN, as they are poisoned. The serpent's conspiracy came into force in a real way because it possessed the power of BLACK MAGIC, which the evil forces did not legally use on EARTH. And people believed in this deception and left the GARDEN. They went to the empty territories of EARTH where they had to find it very difficult to organize them in life and their lives were in danger, as they continued to be followed by evil forces on the EARTH who came to them humanoid animals and continued their plan to destroy these people by killing them in the future. For the first three million years, people lived in danger for their lives, the first mankind was deceived by evil forces and after that, they had to settle on a territory that was not intended for life for people!

The life of the first-created humanity began in the territory of Palestine, but its EARTH consisted only of stone and not intended for human life. People got food and water with great difficulty. There was no water in this territory, as the EMPRESS did not give it there for to stop the existence of these monsters of humanlike animals because they eat humans.

If people did not listen to the snake and did not leave the GARDEN, then nothing have to be happened with the people and the EMPRESS could easily destroy all these monsters that appeared not legally on the EARTH.

But since people were with them in the same territory, the EMPRESS could send people the power of help, the mental protection that humanity enjoys until these days. This is the power of energy that belongs to survival for humanity, belonging to ETERNAL LIFE in a house in the UNIVERSE!

Palestine is the existence of the kingdoms of David and Solomon during the tenth century BCE.

A giant Philistine warrior defeated by the young David, the future king of the ancient Israelites. Facing the Philistines in the Valley of Elah David killed Goliath and saved humanity! David was the messenger of the EMPRESS for to save EARTH from evil spirits. EMPRESS handed over to King David a secret message that was encoded from humanity until its appearance in the future on Earth. Recognize the codes of the EMPRESS, King David does not decipher, but to write down everything that the EMPRESS gave him he could, EMPRESS transmitted the encrypted text he kept in his house. All these secret data in the WILL of the EMPRESS in the future remained preserved under the EARTH of Israel.

And after that, EARTH accepted her WILL!

And the fact that Judge EMPRESS will be is only recognized after 78,000,000,000 billionth. years!

XVIII

PLANETS

All PLANETS have been assigned a new LAW since they all went into a new cycle in my HOME in PARADISE, where they will be in ETERNITY! Under the LAW which only I in full power can change its existence !!!

The LAW has been the force from -

June 23, 2010.

PLUTON _You carry a negative and giving a disagreement in the families of people._

NEPTUNE _You bring to the mankind cheating and made by their hermits._

URANUS _You are closed and not existing for humanity._

SATURN _You have confused people in their homes._

JUPITER _You stopped people's lives._

VENUS _You consolidate the union in love and harmony in people's homes._

MERCURY _You are not a fake and you do the help to achieve the goal for a person to achieve FORTUNE!_

MARS _You give the power to conquer life for people._

MOON _You give power to ETERNAL LIFE in the UNIVERSE HOUSE, you give to humanity LIFE and DEATH IN ETERNITY!_

SUN _You have rayed out a PARADISE LIGHT from now and forever in ETERNITY, which people still did not even know about that never!_

EARTH _You are PARADISE, you are this place for the location of human life in ETERNITY!_

XIX

Penetrating the serpent to the primordial humanity on Earth is caught!

8 August 2006 9:30 pm..

The penetrated snake on EARTH, I caught with the help of my eagle a messenger to EARTH, who carried out my order!

The figure poured by a hot wax is a confirmation that this image shows how a mysteriously powerful eagle flew from an infinite height and on the fly caught a snake that was absolutely weak in order to make any attempts to get away from him!

Ritual with hot wax I did myself personally in order to convey a message to my deceased people in the UNIVERSE.

After that, the curse from the EARTH was lifted at once and humanity was freed from fear of an unknown future on their EARTH!

The territory of the PARADISE is liberated!

Do not think about that what your life will stop on the EARTH! Life on Earth will be in ETERNITY!

EARTH is the home of people!

Details about the existence of human life on Earth I will be reported to you in the future before I leave Earth!

XX

CHURCH "ETERNAL LIFE"

Become one of the founders of the CHURCH "ETERNAL LIFE" what belong to HIGH PRIESTESS from home of the UNIVERSE, where I am at the present time is a QUEEN OF THE UNIVERSE on the Earth and I will talk in my home about the law of the PARADISE! I am WICCAN QUEEN became from the hidden ancient through time with a humanity!

MARGARITA is a Ukrainian - Canadian White witch and author, she represents her supreme justice, extraterrestrial ability to possess energy. She is THE HIGHT PRIESTESS in the UNIVERSE and she informs the whole WORLD that she is the QUEEN of the UNIVERSE crowned by the dead people in the Wiccan Queen on EARTH.

August 2006, the power from above in her majestic Tarot cards informed of the creation of the WORLD and continues to inform about its future.

CONTACT INFO: (FACEBOOK) - QUEEN of the CARDS

https://www.facebook.com/QUEEN-of-the-CARDS-124440124397122/

EMAIL ADDRESS: eternallifewiccan@gmail.com

This is a new church to which all humanity should join in the WORLD! The only church where the LAWS belong to ETERNAL LIFE, these LAWS do not know not one church in the WORLD. Mankind still did not know the truth about the creation of the world. This knowledge belongs only to me since to reach the knowledge of this level the person is blocked from the EARTH!

This is the language of the dead, who have resurrected and will now speak with you, where I will be their leader and pass from them to you all the information that will help you to free yourself from blocking on EARTH with PARADISE. The house which belongs to love in ETERNAL LIFE is located here on EARTH, this house on EARTH will be the only house and church here on EARTH, the church which will be called "ETERNAL LIFE".

For me, there is nothing unmovable.

The organization of the church has an account for cash assistance for which you can contribute your donation so that I can open a room to meet with you in the future since I do not have that much money. The offer of the premises is also accepted.

This is a Wiccan house, what belongs to the QUEEN of the UNIVERSE!

For humanity about the extraterrestrial force was not really been known on EARTH yet, MARGARITA is the only unique person who knows how to communicate with the UNIVERSE from EARTH.

The publication of the CHURCH of "ETERNAL LIFE" has contact with the UNIVERSE, from where you will receive information through guidance in the new church on EARTH.

The UNIVERSE is classified, Margarita has an extraterrestrial power. Sensational discovery of a new science!

* **I** `1-18` QUEEN of the UNIVERSE on the EARTH is QUEEN of the CARDS. The JUDGEMENT DAY.

* **II** `19-58` Declaration of WILL and represents cards. QUEEN of the UNIVERSE is BAPHOMET.

* **III** `59-81` New Tarot card system which is called "THE LAW OF HEAVEN " is Tarot of BLACK MAGIC , the cards have the power of ancient magic and remove hexes of a black witch !

* **IV** `82-85` QUEEN of the UNIVERSE is "GREAT BABYLON".

* **V** `86-90` QUEEN of the UNIVERSE is "WICCAN QUEEN".

* **VI** `91-97` QUEEN of the UNIVERSE is a MARGARITA "THE MASTER AND MARGARITA" (1967), Mikhail Afanasyevich Bulgakov. The novel has been called one of the masterprieces of the 20th century.

* **VII** `98-100` The first book in the WORLD'S about the UNIVERSE which belong to the House of PARADISE. The messages received from those who have already died.

* **VIII** `101-106` The Birth of the Cosmos, where I lived and where was my Home.

* **IX** `107-111` Election of the Path.

* **X** `112-113` There are no other LAWS , other than the LAW of the HEAVEN in the PARADISE.

* **XI** `114-115` Loving soul in ETERNAL LIFE.

* **XII** `116-117` THE LAST TESTAMENT . THE PARADISE PASSPORT of LOVE.

The future of the UNIVERSE and humanity you can learn in the editions from the CHURCH "ETERNAL LIFE" the best publisher.

This book belongs to antiques.

Antiques & Collectibles

www.ingramcontent.com/pod-product-compliance
Lightning Source LLC
Chambersburg PA
CBHW081148020726
47504CB00009B/2029